IN HONOR of BROKEN THINGS

IN HONOR of BROKEN THINGS

PAUL ACAMPORA

Dial Books for Young Readers

Dial Books for Young Readers
An imprint of Penguin Random House LLC, New York

First published in the United States of America by Dial Books for Young Readers,
an imprint of Penguin Random House LLC, 2022

Visit us online at penguinrandomhouse.com.

Library of Congress Cataloging-in-Publication Data
Names: Acampora, Paul, author. | Title: In honor of broken things / Paul Acampora.
Description: New York : Dial Books for Young Readers, an imprint of Penguin Random House LLC, [2022] | Audience: Ages 8–12. | Audience: Grades 4–6. | Summary: "Three unlikely friends meet in a middle school pottery class and learn how to piece their lives back together again, all the while discovering that some things can never be unbroken—and that's okay too"—Provided by publisher. | Identifiers: LCCN 2021031039 (print) | LCCN 2021031040 (ebook) | ISBN 9781984816641 (hardcover) | ISBN 9781984816658 (ebook)
Subjects: LCSH: Teenagers—Juvenile fiction. | Middle schools—Juvenile fiction. | Friendship—Juvenile fiction. | Families—Juvenile fiction. | Pottery craft—Juvenile fiction. | CYAC: Family problems—Fiction. | Middle schools—Fiction | Schools—Fiction. | Friendship—Fiction. | Pottery craft—Fiction.
Classification: LCC PZ7.A17298 In 2022 (print) | LCC PZ7.A17298 (ebook) | DDC 813.6 [Fic]—dc23
LC record available at https://lccn.loc.gov/2021031039
LC ebook record available at https://lccn.loc.gov/2021031040

Book manufactured in Canada
ISBN 9781984816641
1 3 5 7 9 10 8 6 4 2
FRI

Design by Jennifer Kelly
Text set in Calisto MT Pro

For any kid who has ever felt broken

IN HONOR of BROKEN THINGS

Chapter 1

OSCAR

Everything was so easy during the two weeks before my sister died. Her last day was bad, but I don't want to talk about that. Before the very end, we laughed a lot. Carmen had no hair, not even eyebrows. She looked like a pale pink Easter egg, and who doesn't like Easter eggs?

We played a million board games because Carmen loved board games. The hospital had Parcheesi, backgammon, Sorry, checkers, and a chess set without all the pieces. Mom got really upset about the chess pieces. "My kid is literally dying," she said to the hospice nurse near the last day. "How can you give her a game with missing pieces?"

"That definitely seems like a metaphor for something," said Carmen, who was a little punchy from all the medication.

I moved the jelly bean I was using in place of a pawn on the chessboard. "Just play the game."

"Mom isn't wrong about the missing pieces." Carmen took my jelly bean with her bishop. "It's the first thing I'm going to talk to God about when I get to Heaven."

"Who says you're going to Heaven?"

Carmen laughed. "I know I'm going to Heaven because I'm only twelve years old. Even if you do really terrible things, you can't go to the bad place if you don't understand the consequences of your actions, and that's impossible before you are an actual teenager."

I'm pretty sure Carmen could understand the consequences of her actions. I didn't mention that. Instead, I took her bishop with my knight.

"But honestly," she continued. "I'd have liked the opportunity to do some terrible things."

"Maybe don't mention that when you get to Heaven."

"God already knows." Carmen slid a rook across the board, took my knight, and popped the jelly bean into her mouth. "Checkmate."

I never even saw that coming. I reached onto the board and knocked over my king.

Carmen grinned. "Who's dead now, Oscar?"

"It wasn't a fair fight. You're stronger than me in every way."

That made us both laugh because even though I'm just fourteen, I'm already over six feet tall, and I weigh more than two hundred and twenty pounds. Also, I can bench-press two-sixty, and I'm probably the fastest kid at West Beacon Junior/Senior High School whether I'm wearing football pads or not.

"Oscar," Carmen said seriously, "I could snap you like a cracker."

"I know it," I told my tiny pale Easter egg of a sister.

She waved a finger in my face. "Don't you ever forget it."

"I am going to beat you one of these days," I warned her.

We both knew that was a lie.

Carmen died a few days later. She never did any terrible things. I miss her very much. I also miss the days when Mom, Dad, and I simply did anything and everything Carmen asked. Every decision was clear. Every choice was obvious. We didn't worry about school or work or football. The hospital let the three of us sleep in her room. We hardly even ate. We just stayed together.

Now, after a wake, a funeral, the cemetery, and enough tears to fill a backyard swimming pool, Mom, Dad, and I sit alone in our tiny kitchen. The quiet is interrupted when our old refrigerator kicks to life. It hums and shakes when it runs, and a round smiley face magnet falls to the floor. The refrigerator door is covered with get-well notes and prayer cards and recipes for all kinds of different smoothies because smoothies are a very good food choice if you ever have to go through chemotherapy. We'd been looking forward to life without smoothies. But not like this.

"Now what happens?" I ask, because I feel like I'm in one of those slow-motion movie scenes that is very quickly returning to full speed, and I am not ready for full speed.

"Maybe," says Mom, who looks both overdressed and also weirdly sloppy in a long black funeral dress. "Maybe we try to get back to normal."

I know my mother is trying to make me feel better. Dad just closes his eyes and shakes his head. I glance between my parents, who are seated on either side of me. "I'm sorry," I say after a long moment, "but that might be the dumbest thing I've ever heard."

Dad opens his eyes. My father doesn't talk much. Still, I think he's about to yell at me for being rude to my mother. Instead, he takes a deep breath and then offers Mom a very slight smile. "Ana," he says softly. "Oscar might be right."

Mom sits up very straight. "Is that what you think?"

Dad shrugs.

Mom stands and crosses the room. She says nothing. In the corner, she removes a full bag of trash from the plastic garbage can.

"You're going to empty the trash now?" I say.

She heads for the back door. "It's not going to empty itself, Oscar."

"But you're still in a nice dress."

"Don't worry," Mom says as she steps outside. "I'm never going to wear this dress again."

Chapter 2

NOAH

People stare when my mother and I walk into West Beacon Junior/Senior High School. I can't blame them. I am very small, and my mother is very large. Plus, Mom's hair is a wild gray tangle, and she's wearing a giant red lumberjack shirt over a pair of stained blue overalls. Unlike me, she is hard to miss.

"We need to go to the office," I tell her.

Mom ignores me. She's stopped in front of a polished black football that's made out of some kind of stone. It sits atop a wooden pedestal just inside the school's main entrance. Letters engraved on one side of the ball say:

ANTHRACITE BOWL CHAMPS

"Look, Noah." Mom nods at the black trophy. "West Beacon students who do well get a big lump of coal."

I lean forward and read aloud from a framed card attached to the pedestal. *"This Anthracite Bowl Trophy, made from a solid block of anthracite coal weighing two hundred and fifteen pounds, goes to the winner of the Thanksgiving Day football game played annually between West Beacon and Frackville gridiron gladiators since 1925."*

Mom points at the West Beacon mascot, a high-kicking mule, painted on a nearby wall. "If you're lucky, maybe there will be pony rides too."

If I were lucky, we would have arrived at school on time, I would be registered for classes by now, and my mother would not believe in sarcasm as a parenting tool.

"It's not a pony." I drag Mom away from the anthracite trophy and toward the doorway that leads into the school's main office. A moment later, I'm looking over the front desk at West Beacon's school secretary. "Hello," I say. "I'm Noah Wright. I'm here to sign up for eighth grade."

The white woman has a plain face, cat's-eye glasses, and short, unnaturally red hair. She gives me a smile. "I'm Mrs. James, and I know who you are."

I turn to Mom. "Did you call and say I was coming?"

"You're the one signing up to be a Mighty Mule," Mom says. "Not me."

"You won the regional spelling bee," Mrs. James continues. "And the mathletes tournament, and the county art show. I see your picture in the paper all the time. You're Noah Wright."

I nod because we already covered that.

"Aren't you homeschooled?" asks Mrs. James.

"He's decided he wants to come here," Mom informs the secretary. "Homeschool isn't good enough anymore."

I really thought we were done fighting about this. Apparently, we're not.

"Homeschool was fine," I say. "I'm just ready for a change."

"What he really means," Mom says to Mrs. James, "is that he's ready to get out of the house and away from his lunatic mother."

The school secretary smiles and nods. "Mrs. Wright," she says kindly, "*lunacy* is a word that originally referred to a kind of insanity caused by the phases of the moon, but of course there is no such thing. Sadly, and even though the word is meaningless, it can be unkind and even hurtful for people struggling with mental illness, so we don't use it anymore."

"Oh," says Mom.

"Unkind, hurtful, and meaningless," says Mrs. James. "It's not a winning combination, is it?"

"No." My mother is a lot of things, but she is not unkind, hurtful, or meaningless. "I'm sorry."

"Apology accepted." Mrs. James turns to me. "Do you realize that school started a month ago?"

"I'll catch up." I place a fat folder on her desk. "Here's my forms and paperwork for registration along with medical records and a description of my academic progress. I made a list of classes that would work best for me this year. I definitely want to take art. I'm already pretty good in Spanish, but I could use the review. It's probably best for me to take calculus again too."

"Again?" says Mrs. James. "I'm not sure—"

"According to Pennsylvania state guidelines, you have to take me."

Mrs. James gives me a puzzled look. "Why wouldn't we take you?"

"You said you weren't sure."

She looks at me over her glasses. "You didn't let me finish."

"Sorry," I say.

"I'm not sure eighth grade will be right for you," she continues.

"As opposed to what?" says Mom.

"Ninth grade?" says Mrs. James.

"No," says Mom.

"Why not?" I ask.

Mom shakes her head. "You're not getting on a track that ends up with you leaving for college before you turn fifteen."

"I'm already thirteen," I point out.

"I don't care," Mom says. "You're signing up for eighth grade or else you're going back to homeschool."

"Fine," I say, because I don't want to fight with my mother anymore. Plus, I never wanted to sign up for ninth grade in the first place. I push the folder toward Mrs. James. "Everything is filled out and ready to go."

The secretary opens the folder and examines the paperwork. "There's just one parent signature?"

"There's just one parent," I say.

"I'm sorry," says Mrs. James.

"Don't be," Mom and I say at the exact same time.

At least we agree on one thing.

Before the secretary can offer any kind of reply, three girls enter the office followed by a delivery guy pushing a big box on a handcart. Mom rolls up the sleeves on her flannel shirt. "Are we really doing this?" she asks.

"We're really doing this," I tell her.

"In that case," says Mrs. James, "welcome to West Beacon Junior/Senior High School, home of the Mighty Mighty Mules."

Mom raises one hand and twirls a limp finger in the air. "Go Mules." She sounds like she just swallowed a bug.

"It's going to be okay," I tell her.

"You sure about that?"

"I'm sure," I promise, even though I've only been on planet Earth for about forty-eight hundred days, and like most human beings, I spent a bunch of that time pooping in my own pants followed by several years in close relationships with stuffed animals and invisible friends. How am I supposed to be sure about anything?

"I guess we'll see." Mom gives me an awkward kiss on the cheek and then heads for the door.

People stare as she exits the office. I pretend they're

admiring her artsy attitude and quirky fashion sense. I turn back to Mrs. James. "Can I go to a class now?"

"No." The secretary points me toward a chair against the wall. "Sit."

"And do what?" I ask.

"Stay," she says.

I drop into a green plastic chair like a good dog. Around me, the office walls are brown and drab and covered with fading photos of old sports teams. I'm definitely not in homeschool anymore, and everything's going to be fine. At least I hope so.

Chapter 3

RILEY

It's the middle of October, and I have been a West Beacon eighth grader for almost four weeks. I've started every single school day with Mr. Alexander Martin, a skinny white art teacher with a short black beard who leads Introduction to Clay. So far, I don't even wedge—which basically means rolling clay around on a tabletop—particularly well.

Mr. Martin looks over my shoulder while he sips coffee from a handmade mug shaped like a Christmas reindeer. "Working on something for the December art show, Riley?"

I push a strand of hair out of my face. "I'm not sure," I say. Honestly, I'm not really sure about anything anymore.

"You should think about it."

"Is artistic ability required?"

"Artistic ability is not mandatory, but participation counts as your final exam."

"Then I'll think about it."

Mr. Martin throws back a last sip of coffee, then, without looking, he places his ceramic mug atop the pile of papers, pencils, and various clay-making tools that covers his desk. Rudolph the Red-Nosed Coffee Cup stays balanced for a moment, but then it tips and rolls off the desk. Somehow, it drops straight into a plastic pail that Mr. Martin uses for trash. The cup hits the bottom of the bucket and smashes to pieces.

"I meant to do that," Mr. Martin announces.

The class laughs because Mr. Martin is a very nice man. He's also a very clumsy man.

"You should be more careful with your things," a pretty ninth-grade girl named Isabelia tells our teacher.

"No great loss," he says. "That mug was already chipped."

My mother and I moved to West Beacon from Philadelphia near the middle of September. If we smashed all our chipped mugs, plates, and glasses, we'd have to eat off the floor and drink out of the faucet.

"Plus," says Mr. Martin, "I really dislike reindeer."

That's something I can appreciate. One of the first things Mom and I did when we got to West Beacon was run into a two-hundred-pound white-tailed deer. The animal bounced off our front end and sprinted away, leaving us with a crushed bumper, a cracked windshield, and a crumpled fender. I used to think deer were like giant, cuddly bunny rabbits. In fact, they are large, fast-moving, fur-covered bags of cement. As a result, we now drive around town in a beat-up Chevy that looks like it lost a fight with a bulldozer. "Don't worry about it," Mom tells me. "Around here, running into deer is sort of like a hobby."

My mother grew up in West Beacon. She moved us back here after the restaurant where she worked in Philly got robbed. It was just a little diner, and I was there helping out when it happened. A plain-looking man in a bright blue baseball cap came up to the cash register. He smiled, showed my mother a gun, and politely asked for all the money. Mom handed him the cash. The man said thank you. When the door closed behind him, Mom started to shake and cry.

Before middle school, I used to get into fights. I won some and I lost some. Either way, I never let anybody see me cry, but this was a whole new level of scary. As far as I'm concerned, tears are a perfectly good response to a man with a gun. Unfortunately, the owner of the diner, who always seemed nice enough before, disagreed. "Blow your nose," he told Mom. "You're scaring the customers."

Mom's mouth dropped open.

"Did you give away all the money?" he asked next.

Mom looked down and noticed that the cash register drawer, now empty, was still open. She took a breath and slammed the drawer shut. A moment later she announced, "It's time for a change."

Two weeks later, we carried everything we own into a small rented West Beacon row house across the street from Saint Barbara's Catholic Church, which is where Mom's brother, my uncle Pete, is a priest. Uncle Pete greeted us at the door on the day we moved in. "Welcome home," he told me.

"Is that where I am?" I asked him.

Back in the art room, Mr. Martin interrupts my thoughts. "Riley," he says now. "I'm serious about the art show. All students are required to turn in at least one piece by the end of November."

I pick up my clay, which resembles a long gray blob of toothpaste. "Does this look like art to you?"

"Not so much," Mr. Martin admits. "But you've got time."

I drop the clay, which hits the table with a loud *plop.* "All the time in the world isn't going to make me an artist."

"You never know," says Mr. Martin, whose enthusiasm is not always as inspiring as he thinks it is.

A big tenth-grade boy named Aengus looks up from his own clay to see what I've done.

It's kind of weird to be an eighth grader in class with high school kids, but West Beacon Junior/Senior High School is less than half the size of my middle school in Philadelphia, so some classes, like Introduction to Clay, are open to everybody.

"That's a really good snake," Aengus says. He tilts his head. "Or maybe it's a worm?"

For a moment, I am confused, and maybe even a little afraid. Aengus is big and loud, and I honestly don't know if he's being nice or making fun of me. Plus, ever since the robbery I've been wondering if the best solution to being afraid isn't to just punch somebody in the face. It would be tough with Aengus, and it didn't work particularly well in grade school, but I'm willing to try. Even now I wish I could have given the guy who robbed my mother a good punch in the face. Maybe Mom wouldn't have gotten so scared. Maybe she wouldn't have made us run away to the safety of living in the middle of nowhere.

I turn to face Aengus, but Isabelia stops me with a quick smile. "Aengus means well," she says.

I stop, breathe, and then I decide to take Isabelia's word for it.

"Thank you," I say, because first of all, my clay really does look like a snake. Or maybe a worm. Second, I am trying to mean well too.

Chapter 4

OSCAR

I have been absent for thirteen school days, which equals ninety-one class periods, ten thousand tests and quizzes, several tons of homework, and three football games. If I could, I would stay in my room for another week. Or two. Or a hundred. But on the Monday morning following Carmen's funeral, Mom chases me out of bed with a spatula. "Get up!" she yells at me. "You have to go to school."

I pull blankets and a pillow over my head, but that leaves the rest of me exposed. Mom whacks me with the utensil. "Let's go, Oscar!"

I roll out of bed and get dressed because that takes less effort than defending myself against Mom's spatula.

In the kitchen, I sit with my father. He and my mother both work at the Lemko Pretzel Bakery, which has been making pretzels in West Beacon for over a hundred years. Back then, three Lemko brothers came to Pennsylvania from the Ukraine to work in the mines but then realized they liked making pretzels a lot more than they liked digging coal. Now my Mexican American parents work in an old Ukrainian bakery with mostly Dominican coworkers making German-style pretzels that, thanks to the Internet, get shipped around the world. Mom has a job in the front office, and Dad is a supervisor on the production line. I know they've missed a lot of work during the past few months. I can tell because our supply of free pretzels is running low.

I swirl some cereal around in a bowl and drink half a glass of orange juice. Neither Dad nor I speak until I stand and head for the door. "Oscar," my father says just before I leave. "You can do this."

"Thanks," I say, even though I am not really sure what "this" is.

We only live about a mile from school, so I walk most days, which is fine with me. Halfway there, I realize that my parents and I have not discussed football. I have practice this afternoon. Before the season began, people thought West Beacon might have a shot at a state championship this year. Since I've been gone, the Mighty Mighty Mules have lost two out of three games.

I join the crowd of students streaming into the school building. I pass the Anthracite Bowl Trophy, which West Beacon won last year. As an eighth grader, I couldn't play then, but I'm here now. In fact, I spent all summer practicing with the varsity team, and I earned a starting spot as an inside linebacker. Not everybody is happy that a freshman beat out several upperclassmen for the position, which is why I haven't mentioned the fact that I might have dislocated my hip at the end of June. Fortunately, it popped back into place. It still hurts, and sometimes I have to limp a little. Otherwise, it hasn't slowed me down.

Now I head for the office because I assume there must be some sort of reentry requirement after missing nearly half of October. I get in line behind three chatty girls and a brown-shirted delivery man who's pushing a cardboard box on a cart. A short white boy sits in a chair near the wall. He's wearing wrinkled tan pants and a T-shirt that shows a cartoon T. rex playing an old arcade video game called Asteroids.

"Oscar," one of the girls says to me. "Welcome back."

I'm probably supposed to know her. She's blond and blue-eyed. I'm pretty sure that she and her friends are all cheerleaders. "Thanks," I mumble.

"We missed you at the football games."

"It's true," adds one of the other cheerleaders, a dark-skinned Dominican girl. "We couldn't win a single game without you, Oscar."

Are they kidding? Am I supposed to apologize because West Beacon lost a few football games on account of Carmen taking too long to die?

"We're really sorry about your sister," says the third girl, whose hair is long and black and almost unnaturally straight.

Suddenly, I realize that nobody knows what to say when the worst thing in the history of the world happens to you.

Mrs. James, our school secretary, interrupts before I can reply. "Girls," she says sharply. "What are you doing here?"

"We're late for class," one of them says.

Mrs. James passes out tardy slips. "What about you?" she asks the delivery guy.

"I need a signature," he tells her.

She glances at the box. "What is it?"

"It's very heavy." He slides the carton off his cart and onto the floor.

Mrs. James signs a receipt and reads the packing slip. "It's clay." She turns to me. "Oscar, don't you start your day in Mr. Martin's clay class?"

I nod. "I thought I should come here first."

Just then, our principal, Mrs. Ballard, steps into the room. "Oscar Villanueva! We have missed you!"

Mrs. Ballard looks like a short blond scarecrow in heels. Despite a constant smile, she never seems more than two or three seconds away from screaming in some kid's face. For better or worse, she's also West Beacon's biggest football fan, so she's always trying to give me advice about the game. "Oscar," Mrs. Ballard says now. "I am very sorry for your loss."

"Thank—"

She plows ahead before I can finish. "Will you be at practice today?"

"Sure," I say. "But—"

"Friday is a big game."

I nod. "I'll be ready."

I'm not surprised that Mrs. Ballard doesn't take any time to talk about Carmen. If it weren't for football, I don't think she'd ever talk to me at all. According to my mother, Mrs. Ballard's main interest is Mrs. Ballard. "Small-school principals with winning football teams become big-school principals with bigger paychecks," Mom reminds me regularly. "If you didn't play football, that woman wouldn't even remember your name."

"We still have a shot at playoffs," Mrs. Ballard continues. "I know we've lost two games, but with you back on the field, the Mighty Mighty Mules are not out of it."

"Right," I say. "Do I need to get a late slip or anything?"

Mrs. Ballard pats me on the back like we're old pals. "Tell Mr. Martin I said you're fine."

"Wait," says Mrs. James. She points at the box of clay on the floor. "Please take this with you to the art room, Oscar." She nods toward the white boy who's still waiting in the plastic chair. "And take him too."

The boy wearing the dinosaur shirt stands.

"You'll get the rest of your schedule later," Mrs. James tells him.

He nods. "Thank you."

"Oscar?" she says now.

"Yeah?"

Mrs. James comes around her desk and wraps me in a big hug. The top of her head stops below my shoulder, and her arms barely reach around my waist. Suddenly I feel very small, but not in a bad way. "Thank you," I mumble.

She backs away. "Anytime. Now go to class."

I nod and pick up the box of clay. I'm guessing it's no more than fifty or sixty pounds, so I swing it onto one shoulder and then grunt at the dinosaur boy, who is smart enough to know that he should follow.

CHAPTER 5

NOAH

I expected challenges at West Beacon. I didn't think moving through the hallways would be one of them. I squeeze past strangers, dodge open lockers, and stumble over two kids seated in the middle of the floor. "I'm Noah Wright," I tell the giant boy leading me to Mr. Martin's class.

He grunts again and shifts the box he's got balanced on one shoulder.

"Your name is Oscar?"

"How did you know?"

As if anybody in West Beacon doesn't know Oscar Villanueva. Old men in donut shops and regulars at the Beacon Diner already discuss his future at Penn State or maybe Pitt. Everybody expects to see him in the NFL one day too. He's only a freshman, but this is the year he is supposed to lead West Beacon to a Pennsylvania State Football Championship. Plus, kids all around us shout out Oscar's name. They offer him high fives, pat him on the back, and generally make a big deal about the fact that he's in school today.

"Lucky guess," I tell him.

"What's the deal with the dinosaur shirt?" he asks me.

"I like dinosaurs."

"But they're extinct."

I notice a red, white, and green button pinned to Oscar's backpack. At the center of the button, there's a picture of an eagle grabbing a snake. "You've got a dinosaur on your backpack."

Oscar glances at the button. "That's the Mexican flag, and snakes aren't dinosaurs."

"Not the snake," I tell him. "The eagle. Birds are dinosaurs."

"Seriously?"

I nod. "Is your family Mexican?"

"From a long time ago," he tells me. "How do you know so much about dinosaurs?"

"I like to read."

"And talk."

"That too."

Oscar picks up his pace a little. I have to jog to stay with him.

"Are we almost there?" I ask.

"Are you worried you won't make it?"

"I'm worried I won't find my way back."

"It's October," says Oscar. "Shouldn't you know your way around by now?"

I trip over a loose backpack. "Today is my first day at school."

"Where have you been?"

"About six blocks from here."

Oscar turns. Now he just looks confused.

"Homeschool," I explain.

"Since when?" he asks.

"Since forever."

He stops at a doorway that leads into an art room. "This is your first day in real school?"

"Homeschool is real school," I tell him.

"Then why are you here now?"

I could explain that my parents are splitting up, that I don't know where my father lives anymore, that my mother divides her days evenly between sleeping, crying, and raging at the world on Facebook, and, as a result, my home is no longer a very good learning environment. Instead, I say, "It seemed like a good time to try something new."

"Noah Wright," a voice calls from inside the art room. "Is that you?"

I turn and see the teacher, Mr. Martin, smiling at me from the middle of a clay studio. Mr. Martin used to be friends with both my mom and my dad. In fact, Mr.

Martin used to be a regular visitor at our house, but he hasn't been over for months. I can't say I blame him.

"What are you doing here?" he asks.

I step inside the big room, which is light and open and smells like wet dirt. "I'm taking your class."

He laughs. "You're taking Introduction to Clay?"

"I hear you're a good teacher."

"More like a good artist with a healthcare plan. How are your parents?"

My mother hasn't changed her clothes in nearly a week, and I haven't seen my dad since last May. "They're fine," I say. "Thanks for asking."

Oscar lowers the box of clay from his shoulder and drops it in front of the teacher's desk. It lands with a loud thud. "You know each other?"

"Noah's parents are professional potters," Mr. Martin explains. "In fact, Noah could probably teach this class."

"You're an artist?" Oscar asks me.

I shake my head. "I'm not that good."

"You know your craft," Mr. Martin tells me.

"Art is the unexpected use of craft," Oscar offers unexpectedly.

"Oh?" I say.

He points toward a cinder block wall right behind me. "It says so right there."

I turn and see a big bulletin board covered with random

notes and student artwork. Looking closely, I find a postcard with a handwritten note that says: *Craft is what we are expected to know. Art is the unexpected use of our craft*. Nearby, a highlighted passage in a page torn from some book says: *Art wasn't supposed to look nice; it was supposed to make you feel something*.

At my house, art is also supposed to make money. I wonder why that's not on the bulletin board.

"But seriously," Mr. Martin says now, "what are you doing here, Noah?"

"I'm starting school today," I explain.

"At West Beacon?"

I nod. "I said I wanted an art class. They sent me to you."

"You look too small to be an artist," Oscar says matter-of-factly.

I turn and face this giant boy. "Lucky for you, artists come in all sizes."

Mr. Martin clears his throat. "What grade are you in, Noah?"

"Eighth," I tell him.

"But you've probably been doing high school work since you were ten years old."

Oscar drops into a nearby seat. "Are you a genius or something?"

"Noah is not a genius," says Mr. Martin.

"Thanks a lot," I say.

"You've been in homeschool your whole life," Mr. Martin points out. "You've been able to work as fast or slow as you want. Plus, you've been doing schoolwork all year round since forever. Every kid would be further ahead with that kind of schedule."

"Why don't we all do it like that?" asks Oscar.

"Be careful what you wish for." Mr. Martin turns back to me. "Are you really a student here?"

"I am really a student here," I tell him.

"Wow," he says. "In that case, let's get you started."

I look around the classroom, where a dozen other kids are already working. A few are wedging clay into usable material. Others are assembling simple boxes and slab projects. One or two are making coil pots. Nobody's at the pottery wheel, but then I remember that this is Introduction to Clay. I guess I'm going to have to be a beginner again.

CHAPTER 6

OSCAR

Mr. Martin puts me and Noah at a table with a skinny white girl named Riley Baptiste. Riley's got straight blond hair and a round face. She's wearing a loose green Philadelphia Eagles jersey that's almost the same color as her eyes. She's rolling a ball of clay like she's making the bottom half of a very small snowman.

"Excuse me," Noah says to her. "You need to press it down with both hands—"

"That's what I'm doing," Riley snaps.

"You sort of want to squish the clay into the shape of a face," Noah adds.

Aengus Finney, a tenth-grade boy who plays football with me, leans over from a nearby table. "That girl's specialty is worms and snakes."

"There's nothing wrong with worms and snakes," says Noah.

"If that's what you like," says Riley. She stops rolling the ball of clay. "I don't like worms and snakes."

"Noah's parents are potters," I share with Riley. "Maybe he can help."

Riley pokes at her clay with a finger. "Art class at my old school was mostly just crayons and paper."

"You're new here?" says Noah. "I'm new here too."

"I started a few weeks ago. I'm not very good at this." She looks up at me. "What's your story?"

"That's Oscar," Noah tells her. "Everybody knows Oscar."

"I don't," Riley says. "Where have you been?" she asks me.

Without thinking, I close my hands and squeeze a soft ball of clay. It's cool and smooth, and it squishes between my fingers. Somehow the feeling pushes the sudden, terrible burning in my throat and chest away. I take a slow breath and remember that there is no reason for either Riley or Noah to know much about me or anything about Carmen. I breathe again and then answer as evenly as I can. "My little sister died." I focus on the clay. "That's where I've been."

Both Noah and Riley stop working. Unlike most of the people I've run into this morning, they turn their full attention on me. I don't like the feeling of being stared at, but I also appreciate their willingness to not turn away. "When did this happen?" Riley asks seriously.

"It's been ten days."

"And you're already back at school?"

I consider mentioning that my mother chased me out of the house with a spatula. Instead, I just nod.

"My parents are getting a divorce," Noah says now. "I think my mom would feel better if my dad were dead."

"I've never even met my dad," says Riley.

Noah nods thoughtfully. "I wouldn't want to lose a little sister."

"Do you have a sister?" Riley asks him.

Noah shakes his head. "I'm just saying."

I have no idea how to respond to any of this.

Riley turns back to me. "We're really sorry about your sister."

"Thank you." I'm barely able to get the words out. In the meantime, it strikes me that Carmen would probably like these two oddballs, but I'm not sure how to say so in a nice way.

While I struggle to find words, Riley lifts her clay and drops it in front of Noah. "I need help," she announces.

He examines the mess on the table. "You really do," he finally says.

"We're supposed to make something for an art show," she tells him.

I forgot all about Mr. Martin's art show. It's basically the only grade he gives in the class. "When is that due?" I ask.

"We have to have at least one piece ready to show by the end of November," Riley reminds me.

"That's a month and a half away," Noah points out.

"Will you help me?" says Riley.

"I can do that," says Noah.

"Oscar too," she adds.

I sit up a little straighter. "I don't need—"

Riley cuts me off. "What don't you need, Oscar? Help? Friends? Guidance and inspiration from brilliant companions?"

"I guess I can't say no to that."

"No," says Riley. "You can't."

I turn for a moment to stare into sunlight that's streaming through the tall windows at the back of the art room. Outside, the sky is clear, but fat clouds dot the horizon. West Beacon sits inside a northern stretch of the Appalachian Mountains, so the weather can change fast. It's possible to get sunburn, frostbite, and hit by a flash flood all in the same day. I swivel back to Riley and Noah. I didn't even want to come to school today. I definitely did not plan on talking about my sister, learning about dinosaurs on the Mexican flag, or agreeing to a tutor for clay. Apparently, weather is not the only thing that can change fast around here.

CHAPTER 7

RILEY

I see Noah standing by the football-shaped lump of coal outside the school office at the end of the day. He starts jumping up and down and waving. "Riley!" he hollers.

There's a barely noticeable pause in the crowd around us. A dozen different kids look our way, then keep moving. From their expressions, I can see that quickly, wordlessly, they have decided that the excitable boy calling my name is probably a loser. If I go over there, I will be marked as a loser too. I don't want to be a loser.

I am about to turn away, but a hand lands on my shoulder. It's Aengus from clay class. "What?" I ask him.

Aengus nods toward Noah. "I like that kid."

I remember what Isabelia said earlier. Aengus means well. "Yeah?"

"You should go talk to him."

"Why don't you do it?"

"My name isn't Riley."

"Riley!" Noah yells one more time.

Aengus pats me on the back, then heads for the door.

I turn to face Noah. He is still waving and jumping up and down. I sigh, and then I give in. I wade through students who are all leaving the building. It feels as if all these other kids are on their way to someplace that matters. Meanwhile, I am heading toward a small weird boy wearing a cartoon dinosaur on his chest.

"Hi, Noah."

Noah grins, then points at the black football on the pedestal. "How about this for your art show project?"

"I don't think I can win the Anthracite Bowl Trophy for art."

"You don't have to win it. You can make it." He nods at my Eagles jersey. "You like football, right?"

"Of course," I say. "Don't you?"

"Not really."

I have no idea what to say to this. I don't think I've ever met anyone who doesn't like football. I guess it's just one more way West Beacon is not like Philadelphia.

Noah starts walking toward the door, so I follow. Stepping out the front of my old school brought you to an EZ Stop gas station, the Philly Pupuseria y Taqueria, and a tiny cell phone repair shop that also sold candy and ice cream cones. Here, I'm faced with a wide-open lawn, a long, looping driveway, and millions and millions of trees, which cover the mountain ridges that surround the town. Honestly, it's a little overwhelming.

Noah stops on the grass in front of the school building.

"If you don't want to make the football, I could show you how to sculpt a tree."

I remember a poem I had to memorize in sixth grade. It ended with "Poems are made by fools like me, but only God can make a tree."

I am no God.

"How would I make a football out of clay?" I ask.

"You can shape a couple oblong pinch pots and then slip and score them together. From there, it would just be a matter of smoothing the seams, carving out the laces, and then sort of sponging a leather pattern onto the ball. You'll probably have to fire it really slowly so it won't explode in the kiln, but if you get the right glaze, you'll have a perfect coal-black football."

"I only understood about half of what you just said," I tell him.

"I'll teach you," he promises. "When you're done, you can have an Anthracite Bowl Trophy of your very own."

After gunpoint robberies, running away from Philly, making a new home in the middle of nowhere, and who knows what else, I feel like I deserve a trophy. Even if I have to make it myself. "You know what?" I say to Noah. "Let's do it."

CHAPTER 8

OSCAR

By the time football practice is over, my hip is burning, my arms and legs feel like overcooked spaghetti, and I think I'm going to throw up. At the final whistle, I take off my helmet and turn toward the locker room. Before I start off the field, Coach Moyer waves me down.

"Oscar!" the head coach calls. "Come and see me!"

Coach Stanley Moyer is built like a giant white Hershey's Kiss with a patch over one eye and two pretzel sticks for legs. Depending on his mood, he tells us that the eye patch is a result of a car wreck, a combat mission, or a hunting accident. Coach is an endless source of wisdom, rules, and instructions. His advice, which is almost always shouted, includes YOU NEED TWO EYEBALLS TO SEE THREE DIMENSIONS, BUT ONE IS PLENTY FOR PERSPECTIVE! There's also IT'S OKAY TO BE A SLINKY SOME OF THE TIME, BUT IT'S NOT OKAY TO BE A SLINKY ALL OF THE TIME!

Sometimes, it's hard to know exactly what Coach Moyer is talking about. Still, I think he's one of the few people in West Beacon who cares more about me than my all-star football future. Whenever it comes up, he says something like IT'S ALREADY TOMORROW IN AUSTRALIA, AND THEY'RE DOING JUST FINE WITHOUT YOU.

I think he means I should concentrate on what I'm doing today.

One of Coach's biggest rules is IF YOU WANT TO WALK, TAKE UP GOLF. In other words, running is the only appropriate speed on a football field.

I put my head down and sprint his way.

"Oscar," Coach says when I join him on the sidelines. "Have you done a single football-related thing since I saw you last?"

I haven't run or lifted weights or even stretched in over two weeks. I am out of shape, and I'm feeling it now. "No," I admit.

"Don't worry about it," he says. "Tears are sweat for the soul."

That's a new one.

"Is there anything I can do for you or your family?" he asks.

I shake my head.

"I have a sister," Coach adds. "I can't imagine losing her. Do you want to play on Friday?"

It's strange, but talking with a person who always says exactly what's on his mind can be confusing.

"I told Mrs. Ballard I'd be ready."

Coach Moyer's eyes narrow. "Your principal is not your football coach, and that's not what I asked."

"I want to play," I tell him.

"You're sure?"

I nod.

"You think you can't find the treasure unless you fight the dragon?"

"Huh?"

Coach glances up at a pack of dark clouds that have been threatening rain all afternoon. A couple fat drops hit the top of my head like warning shots. A moment later, the sky flashes as if a giant lightbulb just exploded.

"Should we go inside?" I ask.

"No need to ask the question when you're sure of the answer," Coach tells me.

The two of us start toward the locker room, but we're too slow. A deep blast of thunder followed by a massive downpour rolls across the football field. By the time we step into the building, I feel like I've been swimming in my pads. Coach removes his Mighty Mighty Mules baseball cap and squeezes it out like a wet washcloth. In the process, he knocks his eye patch a little out of place.

"How did that really happen?" I ask while he readjusts the covering.

"It was Christmas 1983. My brother Ralphie shot me with his new Red Ryder BB gun."

"That's a movie. I watched it on TV last year."

"It's one of my favorites," Coach admits.

"Are you ever going to tell the real story?"

"Everybody has stories, Oscar. There's no rule that says we have to share them all." Coach Moyer places the Mighty Mules hat back on his head. "I'll be in my office drip-drying. You don't need an invitation to come in and talk."

"Coach?" I ask. "Am I playing on Friday?"

"Didn't we already have this conversation?"

I'm honestly not sure.

"Of course you're playing on Friday."

"Thanks, Coach."

"Good to have you back, Oscar."

At my locker, I sit, kick off my cleats, and pull the rain-soaked jersey and shoulder pads over my head. A couple guys greet me. A few are in the shower. Most are already heading home. Despite my starting position, my place on the team is a little awkward. Some of the older players are still unhappy that I earned a spot that could have gone to one of their friends. The rest of the team looks out for me or, weirdly, looks up to me. Mostly they just give me space and let me do my thing. That's all fine with me because I'm not here to make friends. I treat football like it's my job. I still love the game, and it's definitely fun, but it's also my ticket to a free college education and maybe a million-dollar paycheck one day. I know my parents went through most of their savings taking care of Carmen, so football is going to be a lifeline for us all. I have no intention of screwing it up.

CHAPTER 9

NOAH

"Noah," Mr. Martin says to me on Monday morning. "I hear you had some trouble with your class schedule."

I continue wedging a big ball of clay for Riley. "I got it worked out."

At the end of last week, Mrs. Ballard tried to tell me that eighth graders couldn't take advanced courses. After some discussion, the principal let me register for Honors Biology, AP Calculus, and Spanish III, which are the classes I asked for in the first place.

Mr. Martin takes a long sip from a coffee cup shaped like a pig with wings. "I don't think anybody's ever threatened a lawsuit to get into calculus."

"How do you know about that?" I ask.

Our teacher grins. "There are no secrets inside the West Beacon Junior/Senior High School faculty lounge."

"He means that teachers gossip." Riley looks up from a piece of paper that includes the sketch of a football. "Can I sue to get out of dissecting a frog?"

"No," Mr. Martin tells her.

"But maybe the frog can sue you," I say.

That gets a small smile from Oscar, who is using a toothpick and a knife to sculpt a tiny family of perfect little clay ducklings. He's been hiding the small birds around the room during the week. "My sister liked ducks," he explained when Riley and I caught him at it.

I hand Riley her ball of clay. "I don't know why Mrs. Ballard made picking my classes so difficult."

"Your principal wants this to be a one-size-fits-all school," Mr. Martin explains. "Thanks to your home-school experience, you are not the right size."

Riley nods across the table at Oscar. "Is he the right size?"

Mr. Martin laughs. "Nationally ranked all-state line-backers are always the right size. We're just lucky that our superstar happens to be an authentically good, kind, and smart human being."

"Thanks," Oscar mumbles.

After art, I head to biology and then calculus, which is supposed to be followed by lunch in the cafeteria. Unfortunately, I spent a lot of time getting lost during my first week at school, and I still haven't found the cafeteria yet, so I am very happy to see Riley when I leave math on Wednesday.

"Noah," she calls. "Are you still lost?"

I catch up with her in the middle of the hallway. "How can you tell?"

She points at my T-shirt, which says: I WENT TO THE LAND OF THE LOST AND ALL I GOT WAS THIS STUPID T-SHIRT.

"How was calculus?" she asks.

"It's fun," I tell her.

Riley sighs. "You really are a genius."

"Calculus is just a way to talk about how things change," I explain, then join her as if I'd intended to head that way all along.

Somehow, Riley avoids bumping into people as we move with the crowd heading down the steps. I bounce between shoulders and the stairwell wall like a glass marble falling down a plastic chute. "When you think about it," Riley says, "talking about change is what we do in history, and science, and English lit too. It's like they're all languages." She pauses. "Whoa! I'm having a total insight." She gives me a big grin. "Who's the genius now?"

"You are," I say. "If you can show me how to get to the cafeteria."

"No problemo."

"That's not actually Spanish."

"I don't actually care."

Riley leads us out of the stairwell. We make a quick turn and then stop at our lockers to grab brown-bag lunches. From there, we head down another set of stairs that I didn't even know existed. We finally reach the basement-level cafeteria and find a couple seats at the end of a long table in a back corner.

Riley nods at my lunch bag. "Do you have anything you want to trade?"

"Trade?"

She sighs. "You really don't know anything, do you?"

"I know calculus."

Riley takes my lunch bag and dumps it over. A single banana slides out. "That's it?"

"I make my own lunch."

"You made a banana?"

"I was in a hurry."

Riley reaches into her own bag. One by one, she pulls out a package of cookies, a bag of potato chips, a chocolate bar, and a bottle of flavored vitamin water.

"At least a banana is healthy."

She lifts the water bottle. "This has vitamins in it."

"If you say so." I look around at the surrounding tables, which are all jam-packed with chairs and students. "Who do you usually sit with?"

"Most of these kids have known each other forever," Riley explains. "They already have their own groups. I'm not in any of them."

The cafeteria is definitely filled with some distinct clubs and cliques. In a far corner, a bunch of artsy-looking students appear to be sharing space with an aspiring biker gang. Or maybe those are all theater kids. At the center of the room, several tables hold a big pack of athletic-looking boys and girls. Based on the number of knee braces, they must be West Beacon's jocks. A small group of mostly Black students crowd a table next to some skinny white boys who are all wearing really big headphones. I guess they're gamers or DJs. Maybe both. There's also a large group of Spanish-speaking students who share three tables not far from Riley and me. Right next to us, some serious-looking comic book readers sit beside a cluster of enthusiastic board game players. Whatever they're doing seems to involve dragons, trains, and cats with swords.

"Do you mind if I sit with you?" I ask Riley.

"I can't kick you out now. You're my Play-Doh teacher."

"It's not Play-Doh." I look up and see the third member of our clay club heading toward us from the opposite side of the room. "Here comes Oscar."

"He won't sit with us." Riley says this as if it were obvious.

"Why not?"

"He has to sit with the football players or the Puerto Rican kids."

"What Puerto Rican kids?"

She nods toward the Spanish-speaking tables.

"Most of the Hispanic families in West Beacon are Dominican," I tell her.

"Oh," she says. "I assumed. My bad. Most of the Spanish-speaking kids I knew in Philadelphia were Puerto Rican."

"You're not in Philadelphia anymore."

"Don't worry," she says. "I know."

"Plus," I add, "Oscar's Mexican."

"Mexican American." Riley pops a potato chip into her mouth. "But you're missing the point. Oscar sits with the cool kids. That's not us. And as far as Oscar's family, they're more West Beacon than we are. My mother knows his parents. She thinks Oscar's great-grandparents grew up around here. She remembers your mom from high school too. Small world, huh?"

"Your mother is from West Beacon?"

"My mom and my uncle Pete. You might know him. He's a priest."

"Father Pete? At Saint Barbara's?"

Riley nods. "That's him."

A moment later, Oscar pulls up a chair across from Riley and me. "Can I sit with you?"

Apparently, I'm not the only one who's missing the point.

"Why would you do that?" Riley blurts out.

Oscar takes a step back. "I don't have to."

"Sit down," I say. "We want to ask you a question."

"About what?"

I point at the chair. To Riley's surprise, Oscar joins us.

"Your parents are from West Beacon," I tell him. "My parents are from West Beacon and so are Riley's."

"Just my mom," Riley reminds me.

"Okay," I say, "Riley's mom is from West Beacon."

"And my uncle," she adds.

"Riley's uncle is Father Pete," I tell Oscar.

"At Saint Barbara's?" he asks.

I nod. "The three of us have a lot in common."

"Plus clay," says Riley.

"I like clay," says Oscar.

"But we hardly knew each other at all," I point out.

"What's the question?" Oscar asks.

Honestly, I hadn't thought that far ahead.

"We know you already have a lot of friends," Riley says now.

"Why do you think that?" Oscar asks.

Riley looks around the room. "You can sit at almost any table."

Oscar leans forward. "Do you want to know a secret?"

Riley crosses her arms. "If your big secret is that we can sit at any table too, then I'm going to dump vitamin water on your head."

"That's not what I was going to say," Oscar promises.

"Then what's the secret?" she asks.

Oscar lowers his voice. "I don't belong to any of those groups."

"Of course you do," says Riley.

Oscar shakes his head. "I'm in a new group. It's called the your-little-sister-just-died-and-now-you-sort-of-hate-everybody club."

All of a sudden, it seems as if the noise from the cafeteria fades away, and now Oscar, Riley, and I are sitting somewhere all alone. "That's not a good club," I say softly.

"I know," Oscar whispers.

"You need some friends," Riley tells him.

Oscar begins to open his lunch bag. "That's why I'm sitting here."

CHAPTER 10

RILEY

It doesn't matter where you sit in the West Beacon cafeteria during the week. When Friday night rolls around, everyone has to cheer for Mighty Mighty Mules football.

"We've got home field advantage," I tell Noah during art class, "but Lansford Catholic is supposed to be really good. Plus, their quarterback is related to somebody who played on a team that won the 1925 National Football League championship."

Noah looks up from a pot he's making with a long clay coil. "How do you even know these things? I've lived here my whole life, and I don't know these things."

"I like football." I turn to Oscar. "Noah doesn't like football."

Oscar continues to focus on shaping his clay into a set of small, perfect dominoes. "Why not?"

"I don't like when people get hurt," Noah tells him.

"It's just a game," I say.

"Dominoes is a game." Noah rolls a quick ball of clay

and then, without warning, he slams it down hard enough to make the whole table jump. "That's football."

The clay smash is so unexpected that I nearly fall out of my chair. My heart starts pumping wildly, and I remember how it felt when Mom got robbed. "You scared me!" I yell at Noah, who looks suddenly sheepish.

"I'm sorry," he says.

"You should be! And you should go to the game with me."

"Do I have to?"

"Yes," I insist.

Oscar pushes his clay dominoes aside and turns to Noah. "You never had a chance."

Noah sighs. "Fine."

A few hours later, Noah and I sit in the stands between my mother and my uncle Pete, who's wearing an old West Beacon varsity jacket and a giant foam finger that he waves over his head like a madman.

"SKIN 'EM MULES!!" Uncle Pete screams at the top of his lungs. "MIGHTY MIGHTY MULES KICK BUTT!!"

I have seen people in Philadelphia scream at football on TV and cry while discussing Eagles games that took place before I was born. I had assumed priests would be above all that. As it works out, priests are human too. Or maybe it's just my uncle.

"Lansford Catholic are the Saints," I remind him.

"So?"

"So I didn't know priests could cheer against saints."

Mom laughs. "You don't know much about priests, Riley."

"Or saints," says Uncle Pete.

They're both right. Mom and I are not really churchgoers, and Uncle Pete is the only priest I've ever met.

"Not every saint is worthy," Uncle Pete adds.

"Worthy of what?" I ask.

"Worthy of my support." Uncle Pete turns back toward the game. "GO MULES!!"

Down on the field, our Mules are beating the Saints to a pulp because Oscar Villanueva is a one-man wrecking crew. He hits one Lansford player so hard that the kid's helmet pops off. It rolls from the middle of the field all the way to the end zone.

"Somebody should check to see if there's still a head inside that hat," says Mom, who's got a heavy winter coat over a Beacon Diner waitress uniform. She has to leave after the third quarter to get ready for the restaurant's post-game rush. After football and Boyer's Food Mart, the diner is West Beacon's main meeting place, so Mom's already friends with the whole town.

By the fourth quarter, Lansford Catholic's entire strategy has devolved into simply keeping the ball as far away from Oscar as possible. Unfortunately for them, Oscar is bigger, faster, and stronger than any five Saints combined.

I can't believe this is the same kid who turns stray bits of clay into cute little ducklings. When Oscar hits a ball carrier, it's like watching a sledgehammer smash a pumpkin. He is seriously merciless.

Finally, the referees signal that the game is over. The scoreboard says West Beacon: 35. Lansford Catholic: 0.

Uncle Pete lowers his foam finger. "The Mighty Mighty Mules are back!"

"Or maybe the Saints just aren't very good," says Noah.

"Speaking of saints," Uncle Pete says to Noah, "how come I don't see you at church anymore?"

Noah shuffles his feet. "My mom doesn't really—"

Uncle Pete whacks him with the foam finger. "I'm not talking about your mom. I'm talking about you. Get your butt out of bed and come to eight o'clock Mass on Sunday. Bring Riley, and you can have breakfast at my house afterward."

"Sorry," I tell my uncle. "I have plans."

"What plans?"

"I sleep till noon on the weekends."

"Seriously?" Uncle Pete turns to Noah. "What about you?"

Noah considers the offer. "I do like breakfast."

Uncle Pete uses the foam finger to whack Noah again. "Breakfast isn't the important part."

Noah holds up both hands. "I like Mass too!"

"You do?" I ask. Most of what I know about Mass comes from TV. From what I've seen, it requires sitting still without talking for an hour or more while a priest says some prayers and people sing songs I probably don't like. "What do you like about it?"

Noah shrugs. "It's nice. It's good."

Uncle Pete sighs. "That's not quite the poetry that's inspired people to come to faith for thousands and thousands of years, but I'll take it."

"We'll be there," Noah promises.

"I really don't want to," I tell him.

"I really didn't want to come to a football game," Noah reminds me.

"Then why are you here?"

"Because that's what friends do."

Uncle Pete laughs "Guilting a person into attending Mass is worth a lot of points on the Catholic scorecard."

"Is that what you're trying to do?" I ask Noah.

Noah lets out an exasperated sigh. "I like Mass. Your uncle is a priest. Oscar's family goes too. It seems like something you'd want to try."

"Because that's what friends do?"

"Exactly."

"Plus you get free breakfast," says Uncle Pete.

"Guilt and bribery?" I ask.

Uncle Pete shrugs. "Whatever works."

"I like donuts," I tell him.

He smiles. "I'll see what I can do."

CHAPTER 11

OSCAR

At Saint Barbara's church on Sunday morning, I sit with my parents, stare at the stained-glass windows, and pretend to pray. I'm pretty sure Mom and Dad are doing the exact same thing. It's hard to think of anything besides the fact that Carmen is not here. Once the choir begins to warm up, however, my mind wanders back to the football game. It was the first time I played on our own field since Carmen died. I was nervous about playing in front of the home crowd but then everything got easy once I flattened the first runner. After that, it was a very bad day to be a Lansford Catholic Saint.

Carmen was always interested in saints, but she became sort of obsessed once she got sick. She read all about the saints online, and she could point out their pictures in the stained-glass paintings at church. She even told me how many of them died. Crucifixion happened a lot more often than you realize. Stoning and getting impaled on pointy things was pretty common too. Beheading, burning, hanging, and drowning were also popular options.

"Has there ever been a saint who died in his sleep?" I asked.

"Sure," said Carmen. "But who wants to make a stained-glass picture of some guy napping?"

I shift in my seat and wait for Mass to begin. Once things start, Father Pete will stand on the altar calm and confident like nothing bad has ever happened to anybody. He'll promise that God is with us, that God is present in the world, that God loves us. As far as I'm concerned, Father Pete might be a little too optimistic. Or maybe God is the unreasonably optimistic one. I'm not sure.

My thoughts are interrupted by a sharp elbow in the ribs. I turn and find Riley sliding onto the wooden pew next to me. Noah joins a moment later.

"Hi," Riley whispers.

"What are you doing here?" I ask.

"Noah and Uncle Pete say I'll like it."

I forgot that Father Pete and Riley are related. I wonder if it's weird to have a priest for an uncle.

"And donuts," she adds.

"Donuts are a powerful force for good in the world," says Noah.

I have no idea what they're talking about.

"Good game on Friday," Riley says to me now.

"Thanks."

Mom leans forward and shoots the three of us a look. "Shhh."

"Sorry!" Riley turns her attention to the altar. A moment later, she points at a stained-glass window that shows a woman standing in front of a castle tower. "Who's that?"

"Saint Barbara," I whisper.

Riley sits still for about three seconds, then points at a marble statue of an old white guy holding a spear and an orb. "What about him?"

"Saint Stephen of Hungary," says Noah.

"How do you know he's a saint?"

"Saint Stephen's right hand didn't rot after he died. It's called the Holy Dexter."

Riley gives Noah a skeptical look. "His hand's name is Dexter?"

My father bows his head a little lower than usual.

"*Dexter* is the Latin word for *right-handed,*" Noah explains.

First of all, neither Carmen nor I were interested in saints' body parts, so this is all news to me. Second, homeschool appears to cover a lot more ground than we do at West Beacon Junior/Senior High.

"The Holy Dexter is almost a thousand years old," Noah continues. "It's still in a box in Budapest. You can see a picture on Wikipedia."

"No, thank you," says Riley.

My father laughs. It's the first time I've seen him even smile in weeks.

Riley returns her attention to Saint Stephen's statue. "So why is he hungry?"

Dad's shoulders start to shake up and down.

"Shhhhh!" Mom says again.

"We'll give you a tour of the church after Mass," Noah promises.

Finally, Father Pete, wearing an emerald-green robe decorated with white and gold designs, marches down the aisle and onto the altar.

"Why do priests wear gowns?" Riley whispers.

"It's not a gown," I tell her.

Riley sniffs. "It's not very flattering."

Mom sighs, and Dad laughs again. Apparently, Riley has no idea what's going on, but I can do it all on automatic pilot. I kneel and sit and stand. Noah instructs Riley to stay in her seat when the rest of us go for Holy Communion. Mostly, I stare at the fat puffy clouds that float across the blue sky painted on our church's ceiling. Before I know it, Mass is over. Father Pete walks off the altar, heads down the center aisle, and exits out the back.

"Can the audience leave now?" Riley asks.

"We're not the audience," I tell her.

"What are we?"

I look at Noah. "You explain it."

"We're the church," says Noah.

"Even me?" asks Riley.

"That's up to you," says Noah.

"Isn't it up to God?"

"Father Pete says God opens doors, but it's up to us to walk through them."

Riley looks around at all the statues and stained glass. "What if I want to walk through a door labeled BUDDHIST or EPISCOPALIAN?"

"Then you don't get a donut," Noah tells her.

"What's with the donuts?" I ask.

"We're having breakfast with Father Pete," says Noah. "Do you want to come?"

I look to my parents.

Mom nods. "Go ahead, Oscar."

Noah, Riley, and I move into the aisle. We follow the crowd heading for the church door, but Noah turns aside before we get to the exit. He brings us to a wall covered by a mural the size of a small billboard. The painting shows a tall robed woman holding a golden glowing cup that illuminates the inside of a stone cavern. Around her, broken wooden beams and shattered rocks have collapsed and partly buried a group of bloody, injured men.

"This is another picture of Saint Barbara," Noah says to Riley.

Riley studies the woman who looks like a cross between the Statue of Liberty, Miss America, and the kind of angel you'd stick on top of a Christmas tree. "What is she doing?"

"Saint Barbara is the patron saint of coal miners."

Noah points at the image of a man reaching toward the saint. "That's my great-grandfather."

Riley looks shocked. "This is from real life?"

Noah nods. "A mine explosion trapped half a dozen men inside a collapsed tunnel just north of town in the 1920s. The miners started to pray, and a woman appeared to them. She showed them to a crosscut and an underground stream that led outside. My mom says her grandfather always believed it was Saint Barbara and that she saved him for some purpose."

"What did he do after that?" asks Riley.

"He went back to the mines," Noah tells her.

"If a saint ever shows up to save me, I'd really have to think about changing my life."

"Why wait?" says Noah.

Riley considers this. "That's a good question."

The three of us continue wandering through the rest of the little church. We admire stone sculptures, stained glass, and the tall marble columns that hold up the roof. "Can I ask something?" Riley says after a little while.

"Sure," says Noah, who seems to know a lot of things about a lot of things. "What is it?"

"When do we get breakfast?"

We head outside and walk beneath a giant red oak still filled with yellow, green, and copper-colored leaves. Noah leads the way to a rusty iron gate, which opens to Father

Pete's front steps. At the door, Riley presses a brass doorbell, and we wait.

Nothing happens.

Noah leans forward and pushes the bell again. Still nothing. We know Father Pete is in there, so we take turns pressing the button again. And again. And again.

Suddenly, the door swings open. A little old white lady scowls at us across the top of an aluminum walker. "Do I look like Usain Bolt to you?" she asks.

"What?" says Noah.

"Who?" asks Riley.

The woman leans on her walker and points a hand toward the sky in an awkward victory pose. "Usain Bolt!"

"Usain Bolt is one of the greatest sprinters of all time," I tell my friends.

The old lady raises her hand a tiny bit higher. "Do I look like Jamaican Lightning?"

"Usain Bolt's nickname was Jamaican Lightning," I explain.

"I am not Jamaican Lightning!" the old lady adds in case we are not aware of it. "I am an old Polish woman filled with arthritis and sciatica, but people ring that bell like I'm some Olympic superstar waiting to hear a starter pistol so I can drop everything and race to the front door because you think I have nothing better to do."

Without warning, the woman turns, swings her walker

around, and marches back into the house. Every one of her steps sounds like it has an exclamation point tacked onto it.

"Now what?" Riley whispers.

"I think we're supposed to follow," says Noah.

"Are you coming?" the Polish lady yells.

"Let's follow," I suggest.

We head down a hallway behind this woman who is not Jamaican Lightning. She brings us to a bright, sunlit kitchen, where we find Father Pete. He looks up and smiles over a big cup of coffee. "Where have you been?"

"They were showing me the church," Riley tells her uncle. "Is it okay if Oscar comes for breakfast?"

Father Pete points at his kitchen table. It's covered with fresh fruit, stacks of waffles, a couple big pitchers filled with orange juice, and a big pile of homemade donuts. "Mrs. Czarnecki made more than enough for all of us."

"I hope so," says the old woman, who I guess is Mrs. Czarnecki.

"I'm sure of it," Father Pete tells her.

"In that case," she says, "I'm heading home." Without another word, Mrs. Czarnecki and her aluminum walker make a quick U-turn and leave the room.

"Is it me?" says Riley. "Or is that lady a little scary?"

Father Pete laughs while Riley, Noah, and I join him at the table. "Mrs. Czarnecki was still bow-hunting during bear season until a couple years ago."

Riley's eyes go wide. "She hunted bears with a bow and arrow?"

Father Pete starts passing plates around the table. "You're not in Philadelphia anymore, Riley."

"That's what I've heard. Are there really bears around here?"

"Don't leave any porridge out, and you'll be fine."

Riley takes a donut. "Thanks for the advice."

Father Pete sips his coffee. "So what do you think about our little church?"

"It's like a museum," says Riley.

"No," says Father Pete. "A museum is a collection of things. A church is—"

"A collection of saints?" says Riley.

"Saints-in-training." Father Pete bites into a donut and then speaks through a mouthful of sugar and jelly. "And I think we're more of a community than a collection."

"I liked Saint Barbara," Riley tells him. "She was like a superhero down in those coal mines."

"The miners certainly thought of her that way." Father Pete takes another sip of coffee. "Saint Barbara is also a patron saint of fireworks, firefighters, mathematicians, and a good death."

"A good death?" I think of Carmen as well as all the dead saints pictured on the stained-glass windows inside the church. "What's a good death?"

The priest nods thoughtfully, then places his mug on

the table with a loud clunk. "Oscar," he says, "a good death is any one that has been preceded by a good life."

I think about my sister's weeks and months and years. She laughed a lot. We played a million games. She beat me more often than not. I know she had a good life. There just wasn't enough of it.

CHAPTER 12

NOAH

When we can't eat any more, Father Pete makes Oscar and me fill a couple brown paper bags with the remaining donuts. "Take them home for your parents," he tells us.

"What about me?" Riley asks.

"You're family," he says.

"Family gets nothing?"

"I'll have Mrs. Czarnecki make a special batch just for you," Father Pete promises.

"I don't like donuts enough to risk getting struck by Polish lightning," Riley tells him. She's joking, but there's something in the tone of her voice that sounds angry, or at least disappointed. I don't think Riley likes getting left out of things.

After we thank Father Pete and say our goodbyes, Riley, Oscar, and I stop on the sidewalk before we go our separate ways. The sun is higher now and the sky is as blue as the cerulean glaze Mom likes to use when she makes flower vases and fruit bowls. Without speaking, Oscar pulls a spare paper bag from a back pocket. He unfolds it, shakes it open, and then adds two fat honey-glazed donuts from his own leftovers. He nods toward me, and I hand over an apple-cinnamon plus a blueberry cake.

"Family gets nothing," says Oscar, "but friends share."

Riley opens her mouth, but nothing comes out.

Oscar pushes the bag toward her. "Take it."

"But—"

Oscar cuts her off. "You're welcome."

Riley grins, accepts the gift, and then jogs across the street to one of the run-down, two-story row houses that face Saint Barbara's. Some have curtains on their windows. Some don't. Most need new shingles and gutter repairs. Riley's is a slant-roofed box with fading yellow siding and a screen door that doesn't close all the way. Riley steps halfway into the house, then turns back and gives Oscar and me a quick wave before ducking inside.

"That was nice of you," I say after a moment.

"It's what I'd want you to do for me," he says simply.

The two of us walk a block together without speaking. Even though it's a pretty day, we're the only people outside. There aren't even any cars. Once upon a time, these streets and sidewalks were packed. A hundred years ago, West Beacon had more residents per square mile than New York City. Everybody came because of the coal mines. Whether you were a miner, a barber, a carpenter, a cook, a doctor, a bookkeeper, or a maid, the mines created jobs for everyone. Only people with injuries or disease went without work. Of course, life without work in a coal town generally meant no life at all. "Work, leave, or die," Dad used to say when we talked about the history of our town. "Those were your choices."

"Where do you live?" I ask Oscar when we reach the corner of Church and Water Streets.

Oscar points downhill toward the narrow Beacon Creek. The little brook runs between rows of tiny houses built years ago by the mining company for immigrant workers. The water, which cuts across the bottom of a hillside cemetery and then bends around the north side of our school grounds, runs crystal clear thanks to leftover chemicals that still drain from old mines. The runoff kills all the bacteria and microscopic life that usually turns streams cloudy.

"Are you near the creek?" I ask.

"Pretty close," he says. "I used to beg my parents to let me swim in it."

"I tested the water quality of that creek for a science fair project once. Nobody should swim in it."

"I know," says Oscar. "I thought swimming in the chemicals would give me superpowers."

"Chemicals don't actually do that."

"How do you know?" he asks.

"Science," I tell him.

He laughs, which surprises me because I've never heard

him laugh before. "It doesn't matter," he says. "Superpowers are overrated."

"How do you know?" I ask.

"Comic books," he says seriously. "See you tomorrow, Noah."

Oscar turns downhill. I head in the opposite direction. After a few steps, I look back. Oscar is already out of sight, so I tuck my hands in my pockets and head up the hill toward my own neighborhood. It's almost noon, so my mother might be out of bed by the time I get home.

When Dad left in the spring, he promised that he and I would hang out every other weekend, but I haven't seen him once. He emailed in August to say he'd joined the art department of some college near Pittsburgh. I already knew that because I started opening Mom's bank statements and paying our bills after the Internet got shut off for a week in June. I discovered that my father puts part of his paycheck directly into our checking account every two weeks, so I guess that's something.

I lean forward into the breeze and think back to the options that, according to my father, are the only ones available in West Beacon. Work, leave, or die.

Dad made his choice. Mom hasn't picked yet. I'm not sure what that means for me.

CHAPTER 13

RILEY

The screen door slams behind me, but it doesn't latch. I ignore it because I've wrestled with that door for weeks, and I never win. Also, I don't really want to look back and see Oscar and Noah checking out our dumpy house.

"Riley," Mom calls from the kitchen. "Is that you?"

"It's me." I find Mom at the table, where she's playing a word game on her phone. It's what she does to relax. She's also got some kind of salsa music blasting from an old plastic radio on the counter. "What are you listening to?"

"This station used to play polka when I was a kid."

"That's not polka music."

"I know," she says. "But I like it. Where were you?"

"I had breakfast at Uncle Pete's with my friends."

"The Villanueva boy?"

"And Noah Wright." I turn the radio volume down a little and then drop into a chair. "We went to Mass."

Mom looks up from her phone. "Oh?"

I put my donuts on the table. Mom reaches over and takes a honey-glazed. "Mass, huh?"

I nod.

"What made you do that?"

I point at the bag. "Bribery."

Mom bites into her donut, then uses a sleeve to wipe crumbs off her face. "These are homemade."

"I might go to Mass again just for the donuts."

"Let me know," Mom says through a mouthful. "Maybe I'll join you."

I remember what Noah told me. "Donuts are a powerful force for good in the world."

"Excuse me?"

"Never mind." Even though I have new friends and fresh donuts, and I even like that Uncle Pete is nearby, I'm still sort of mad at my mother. It would have been nice if she had at least asked for my opinion before running away from our old home and turning my entire life upside down. I stand and turn the volume back up on the radio. "I'm going to work on some school stuff."

Mom turns back to her word game. "Let me know if you need help."

I grab a donut and head upstairs to my room.

Our little house has just two bedrooms. Mine has just enough room for a twin bed, a chest of drawers, and not much else. I plop onto the bed, grab a notebook from the folding tray table I use as a nightstand, and open to a page where I've been sketching footballs. So far, my plan for making a clay version of the Anthracite Bowl Trophy has not gone well. Mostly, my pieces have collapsed and come out looking like crushed loaves of bread. Based on my early attempts, it's hard to believe I've ever even seen a football.

"A football is a prolate spheroid," Noah informed me during one of our lunch periods earlier in the week. "That means that the polar radius is greater than the equatorial radius."

Oscar, who joins our table every day now, dumped a bag of pretzels onto his cafeteria tray. "I think Noah just said that a football is longer than it is wide."

Noah nodded. "Exactly."

"I already knew that," I told him.

"Did you know that an inflated pig bladder is a prolate spheroid?" Noah asked.

Oscar lifted a hot dog that he'd purchased for lunch. "I'm trying to eat here."

"I guess that makes sense." I read somewhere that footballs used to be made out of inflated pig bladders. "But footballs aren't made with pig bladders anymore."

Noah shook his head. "Now they're just rubber balls wrapped in calfskin leather."

"Calfskin?" I asked. "Not pigskin?"

"It never was pigskin," said Noah. "You can look it up."

Oscar lowered his hot dog. "Are you done?"

"When you think of it," Noah told us, "a football is just a really tough hot dog."

Oscar threw the rest of his lunch away.

Noah must be rubbing off on me, because I went ahead and did more reading. Now I know more about footballs than ever. In addition to having very specific dimensions, all NFL footballs are hand sewn in an Ohio factory that's surrounded by wide-open fields of corn and soybeans. Making the football involves a secret process that requires leather that has to come from cows raised in Iowa, Kansas, or Nebraska. I hoped that knowing every possible thing about footballs would make it possible for me to sculpt one of my own. As it works out, art is more complicated than that.

In fact, I can barely even draw a football on the page yet. I put my notepad aside and fall back on my pillow. I stare at a crack that stretches across my ceiling like the long arc of a Hail Mary pass. According to my research, physicists estimate that a thrown football's "bounce geometry" can lead to more than a million possible outcomes once the ball hits the ground. In other words, anything can happen, which means that it's how a player reacts that really matters most.

From downstairs, Mom's radio continues to play Spanish-language dance music. My mind wanders back to the day of the robbery. I remember hearing a Phillies baseball game from the radio in the kitchen. There were a few customers, but none had a clear view of the cash register. Nobody knew what was happening except for Mom, me, and the man with the gun. Anything could have happened. And I did nothing. I was frozen in place. I never want to be frozen in place again.

CHAPTER 14

OSCAR

On Monday morning, I can hardly move through the hallways at school because everybody wants to slap me on the back and trade high fives. Mrs. Ballard actually stops me outside Mr. Martin's classroom to give me a hug.

"Oscar Villanueva!" the principal yells.

As politely as possible, I twist out of her grip. "Yes?"

"Oscar Villanueva!" She has to shout over the sound of the bell announcing the start of first period.

"That's me."

Mrs. Ballard is so excited that she's hopping from one foot to the other. I'm a little worried she might trip and fall into one of the display cases that Mr. Martin fills with student artwork. "How is our star player this morning?" she asks.

My ribs are sore, my ears are ringing, and my sister is still dead. "Fine," I say.

"We are on the road to a state championship, Oscar!"

"I just want to get to class," I tell her.

"Don't worry about that. How about that game on Friday?"

I know we won. I don't remember the final score, but I do recall hitting a few kids harder than I needed to. I hope nobody got hurt.

"It was good, I guess."

"You guess? It was better than good. It was great. Really great!"

For a moment, I am seriously afraid that this woman is going to head-butt me just for the fun of it.

"Mrs. Ballard, I don't want to be late." I've been thinking about possible projects for the art show, and I want to talk to Noah and Riley about it.

"For clay class?" she asks.

I nod.

Mrs. Ballard rolls her eyes. "Then you better go!"

She offers me a fist. I reluctantly bump it with my own.

"Go get 'em, Oscar! GO MULES!"

"Okay." I back away slowly because it seems to me that Mrs. Ballard along with most of my classmates and maybe all of West Beacon have lost their minds. They've invented a story for how the Mighty Mighty Mules' football season is supposed to go. Whether I like it or not, I am supposed to be the star of their show.

CHAPTER 15

NOAH

Class has already begun by the time Oscar joins Riley and me at our worktable in the art room. "Where have you been?" I ask.

"Hell," says Oscar.

Riley looks up from a wad of clay that she's torturing. "What is that supposed to mean?"

"I had to hug Mrs. Ballard."

Mr. Martin, who is standing nearby, laughs out loud. "A trip to the underworld is an important part of a hero's journey, Oscar. I hope you're able to rejoin the land of the living."

"I'm here now." Oscar narrows his eyes and stares at a ball of clay that I've molded into the shape of a skull. "What's that for?"

"The Day of the Dead," Mr. Martin explains. "It's next week. The decorated skulls are a traditional part of Día de los Muertos celebrations, so I've asked everybody to make one of their own."

I use the tip of a sharp knife to trace a line of teeth into my skull's jaw. "The skulls are called calaveras."

"I know what they're called," says Oscar.

"More than one-third of West Beacon's student population speaks Spanish at home," Mr. Martin informs us. "The art curriculum should represent our community."

Isabelia raises her hand. "Mr. Martin, Day of the Dead is not a big deal in the Dominican like it is in Mexico."

"Oh?" says Mr. Martin.

"We might all speak Spanish, but we're not all the same."

"Of course," says Mr. Martin, who is obviously embarrassed. "I'm sorry. I guess a better teacher would have known that."

"But a worse teacher wouldn't have apologized," Isabelia tells him. "So you'll do."

Mr. Martin smiles. "Thanks."

At our table, Oscar takes a piece of clay and pounds it into the shape of a square. He continues wedging and pushing and pulling until the clay is smooth and free of air bubbles. From there, he rolls out a long, slender tube a little thicker than a person's thumb.

"What are you doing?" I ask.

"I'm not making a calavera," he says.

Riley looks up from her own uneven ball of clay. "Why not?"

Oscar continues working. "We never did any of the Día de los Muertos things when I was little, but then my sister saw that movie *Coco.*"

"The one with the cartoon kid who doesn't want to make shoes?" says Riley. "And then he has all these Mexican musical adventures with his grandfather and his ghost dog in the Day of the Dead spirit world?"

"That's the one." Oscar uses a piece of wire to slice his clay into a set of short cylinders.

"Seriously," I say. "What are you doing?"

"I'm making a chess set for the art show." Oscar counts out his clay pieces and then proceeds to cut a few more. "Carmen loved chess."

We've known each other for two weeks, and it strikes me that this is the first time Oscar has shared his sister's name with us.

"She used to make me and my parents cut out paper skeletons and then set up little Day of the Dead altars with snacks and gifts for our grandparents. The funny thing is that our grandparents aren't even dead. They're retired, and they live in South Carolina. Carmen used to say it was okay because they'd die one day." Oscar pauses. "Who knew she'd beat them to it?"

Riley stops working on her calavera. Together, we watch Oscar organize a set of small clay cylinders on the table.

"Not only that," he continues, "my dad says Carmen

might be the first person in his family to ever even celebrate Day of the Dead. My father's great-great-great-grandfather was a Mexican ranch hand who got drafted to serve in a Texas regiment during the Civil War. He fought at the Battle of Gettysburg and then never went home. Día de los Muertos was not a big deal back then."

"Especially not in Pennsylvania," I say.

"Not in Mexico either," says Oscar.

"What side of the Civil War was Texas?" asks Riley.

Oscar lines up his clay pieces like toy soldiers. "The wrong side."

Mr. Martin wanders back to our table and looks down at our work. "What's going on here?" he asks.

"Oscar's not making a skull, and I have no family history," says Riley.

"Your family is from here," I remind her.

"All I know about is my mother and my uncle," she says. "My father's never been around, and we never talk about my grandparents. If I have a family tree, then I'm on a branch that got snapped off and thrown into a compost pile."

"America is the world's compost pile," says Mr. Martin.

"Do you mean melting pot?" I ask.

Mr. Martin shrugs. "Something like that."

"It's actually nothing like that. The melting pot is a myth from when people wanted to believe that America meant everybody should sort of be the same."

Oscar shoots me a quick grin. "Homeschool strikes again."

"I don't think everybody should be the same," Mr. Martin insists.

"Nobody does," I say. "Probably nobody ever did." I turn to Riley. "America is more like a box of broken sticks than a compost pile."

She laughs. "In that case, my family fits right in."

Mr. Martin puts a hand on Oscar's shoulder. "But you still owe me a skull."

The teacher walks away, and Riley lifts her calavera, which looks like a gourd with a face. She offers it to Oscar. "Do you want mine?"

"I'll do it," he mutters quietly.

Riley adjusts her clay skull a little bit more. Now it looks like a lopsided Mr. Potato Head. She points at my own calavera, which, I have to admit, is awesome. "How did you get so good at this?"

"Both of my parents are artists," I remind her. "Every one of my lessons had art in it. According to my mom and dad, art is the answer to every question and the solution to every problem."

Riley looks at the messy lump of clay in her hands. "I really hope that's not true."

"If art solved everything, then my parents would still be married." I stick my finished calavera onto the end of a pencil. "But they're not."

We're interrupted by Mr. Martin. "Ladies and gentlemen, if I can have your attention for a moment."

We all turn to face our teacher, who takes a clay sculpture from Aengus. The piece, which is the size of a small melon, looks more like a miniature football helmet than a skull. Still, Aengus is proud of his work. "I made that!" he announces happily.

"And we are all very impressed," says Mr. Martin.

The class laughs because it's basically impossible to dislike Aengus.

Mr. Martin lifts the skull a little higher and then reads to us from a textbook he's got open on his desk. *"El Día de los Muertos is a day to celebrate and remember and even visit with family who have passed over to the land of the dead. It's a way for all of us, dead and alive, to continue helping one another on our journey. Calaveras, from the Spanish word that means 'skull,' are often made out of sugar to remind us to enjoy the sweetness of life before we die."* He looks up from the book and smiles at the class. "That's why it's time for candy."

A moment later, Mr. Martin is walking around and giving out marshmallow Peeps from a big plastic jack-o'-lantern. Isabelia leans toward Oscar. "Is this how they do it in Mexico?"

"I have no idea," he tells her.

I guess this is Mr. Martin's attempt at being multicultural, but it really makes no sense at all. Just the same, nobody refuses Peeps.

When the teacher gets to us, I point at the clay cylinders still lined up on our worktable. I can see what Oscar's trying to do, but the pieces are not shaped evenly or sized well. It's going to be difficult to mold them into anything that actually looks good. "Oscar wants to make a chess set," I explain to Mr. Martin. "I think he'd have better luck on the pottery wheel."

Mr. Martin tucks his plastic pumpkin under one arm. "We don't generally use the wheel as part of Introduction to Clay," he says. "But—"

Before Mr. Martin can finish, Oscar stands, gathers all his clay pieces, and squishes them into a ball. "It's fine."

"Oscar?" says Mr. Martin.

"What are you doing?" I ask.

Oscar pushes his chair away from our table, crosses the room, and drops his clay into the plastic trash bucket we use for recycled material. The whole class is staring now. "I have to go," he announces.

"Where?" says Riley.

Oscar shakes his head. He doesn't answer, and he seems suddenly out of breath.

"Oscar?" says Riley. "Are you okay?"

But Oscar is already out the door. Riley looks stunned, and I have no idea what just happened.

CHAPTER 16

OSCAR

I'm not sure where to go after I leave art class, so I head for a restroom. Unfortunately, the West Beacon Junior/ Senior High School toilet facilities are disgusting. I don't last even five minutes in there. I return to the hallway, but I can't go back to the art room. I know Mr. Martin means well, but I'm just not ready for a celebration of the dead.

I turn away from the classroom and walk through the hallways as if I have someplace important to go. It's the middle of the period, so the corridors are empty. Without exactly meaning to, I find myself facing a set of double doors that lead outside. It would be so easy to just leave for the day. I put my hand on the door handle, but I am interrupted by somebody calling my name.

"Oscar?" Mrs. James, our school secretary, stands just a few feet away. She bends over a water fountain, takes a quick drink, then wipes a sleeve across her face and gives me a smile. "Good game on Friday."

I nod. "Thank you."

"Mr. Martin called the office and let me know you'd stepped away from his room for a moment."

"Yes." It's all I can think of to say.

"Are you going back to class now?"

"I'd rather go home," I admit.

She nods. "I see."

The two of us stand without speaking for a long moment.

"Here's the thing," Mrs. James finally says. "If you leave the building it's going to become a big deal. It'll appear as if you cut class and then skipped school. I'd have to call your parents. There would be detention. Maybe suspension. If that happened, you wouldn't be allowed to play football this weekend."

Outside, there is sunshine and blue sky. The morning air is probably still cool and crisp. Staying in school definitely feels like the less sensible choice.

"I'm not going back to class," I tell her.

"You have other options."

"Like what?" I consider the double doors leading outside. If I go through them, I'll end up on the far south side of the school, which means I'll have to walk all the way around the building—and beneath the windows of a dozen different classrooms—in order to head home. I've already had enough people look at me today.

"Does this have something to do with your sister?" Mrs. James asks now.

"Mr. Martin is passing out candy for Day of the Dead."

"Too soon, huh?"

I nod.

Mrs. James steps toward me, puts a hand on my back, and turns me away from the exit. "Come and keep me company, Oscar."

I give in.

Slowly, we walk through the empty hallways. We stop at my locker so I can get some books. I grab my gym bag too, but Mrs. James stops me. "Sorry, Oscar. No football today."

"I can't miss practice, Mrs. James."

"You also can't walk out of class, and yet—"

"When you miss practice without a good reason, Coach Moyer gives you PIE."

"Pie?"

"Personal Improvement Exercises. It's usually three hundred yards of bear crawls, leap frogs, and sprints, but he almost always tacks on another hundred yards if you're a starter."

"PIE," says Mrs. James. "I'll have to remember that."

"So can I go to practice?"

Mrs. James pats me on the back. "You really can't."

I'm afraid I will be eating a lot of PIE tomorrow.

Back in the office, Mrs. James parks me inside a small, windowless conference room down the hall from her desk. "Do some homework," she tells me. "I'll let you know when to come out."

It's still early on Monday morning, so I don't actually have any homework yet. Just the same, I open my math book and struggle through several problems. I spend a bunch of time with history, biology, and Spanish chapters too. People always expect that my Spanish will be excellent. As it works out, skin color is not an indicator of language skills. In other words, mi español es no bueno.

After lunch, Mrs. James steals a slice of birthday cake for me from the faculty lounge, and I spend the rest of the afternoon reading *The Grapes of Wrath*. Our English teacher says the book is about the great American search to find a good life. I don't know how that's even possible when someone or something is dying on every other page. The novel actually starts with a turtle getting run over by a truck on the highway. The turtle doesn't die, but still. I don't know what the author was thinking.

When the bell finally rings, I gather everything back into my bag. I wait a few minutes, but nobody comes to set me free. Finally, I leave the small room and head to Mrs. James's desk. She's not there. She's probably putting out a fire or finding the principal or helping another kid who's about to make a bad decision. I decide to take my chances and leave for the day.

I hurry through an empty hallway and exit the building. Outside, the sun is high in the sky. Kids are catching rides, hopping on bikes and skateboards, or just walking home. I hear somebody call my name. I'm pretty sure it's

Noah, but I don't want to talk. I pull my sweatshirt hood over my head, slip between two yellow buses, then lower my chin and break into a jog across the narrow road running in front of the school.

I don't remember exactly what happens next. A car horn blasts. There's a hard thump. It sounds like a fist punching a sofa pillow. I think that's my body hitting the pavement. This must be how that dumb turtle felt in *The Grapes of Wrath*. Out of nowhere, I recall one of Carmen's favorite jokes.

Why did the squirrel cross the road?

It was stapled to a chicken.

Unlike the squirrel, the chicken, or the turtle, I never make it to the other side.

CHAPTER 17

RILEY

It's easy to find Mom in the line of cars waiting at the curb after school. Not only does our Chevy feature a deer-shaped indent stamped into one fender, but my mother is also the only person blasting big band music while she waits for me to get out of class.

"What are you listening to?" I ask when I slide onto the front seat.

"Oldies station." Mom taps out a beat on the steering wheel. "This is Jimmy Dorsey and his orchestra. The Dorseys grew up just a few miles away."

I want to talk about what happened with Oscar this morning, but I can see that Mom's worn-out from working back-to-back shifts at the diner today. Her hair, usually wrapped in a tight blond bun is loose and unruly. She's still wearing her waitress uniform, and her nametag—HELLO, I'M SUZY—is pinned on upside down. I guess my stuff can wait.

I buckle my seat belt. "Were you and Jimmy friends?"

"Jimmy who?"

"Jimmy Dorsey."

"Riley," says Mom. "The man died before I was born."

How was I supposed to know?

A moment later, Jimmy Dorsey wraps things up, and a new song begins. Now we're listening to a high-pitched girl yodeling along to a guitar-and-fiddle country tune.

"Yee-ha!" says Mom. She begins to sing along at the top of her lungs. "*Yodel-a-ee-he-he . . . He-he-he-he-he-he!*"

I reach for the radio knob, but Mom slaps my hand away.

"The windows are open!" I protest.

"I've been working all day, and now I want to sing."

"You're not even singing real words." I turn down the radio. "Pay attention to the road."

"Riley," says Mom. "You're the one distracting me."

She turns the volume back up, starts the car, and shifts into gear. I don't know if it's the yodeling or the extra gas or maybe a little reindeer spirit rubbed off on our bumper, but the old sedan surprises us by leaping away from the curb. This car has never leaped before. Ever. Unfortunately, the Chevy decides to channel its inner NASCAR just as somebody steps into the road from between two buses. Mom slams on the brakes and the horn at the same time. The radio girl continues to yodel. I think she's singing a song about mules. A boy, now directly in front of us, turns and stares at me through the windshield.

"Oscar!" I shout.

There's a *screech!* followed by a loud *thump!* Oscar crumples to the blacktop. I jump out of the car and see Oscar on the ground clutching his leg. He must be in shock because he's yelling, "I'm okay! I'm okay!"

He doesn't look okay.

At some point a police car, an ambulance, and Mrs. Ballard all join the scene. "He says he's okay," Mrs. Ballard yells. "He says he's okay!"

I really don't think he's okay. The paramedics must agree, because they strap Oscar onto a stretcher and load him into the emergency vehicle. For some reason, Mrs. Ballard hops into the ambulance too. "Positive thoughts!" she shouts at us before they close the rear doors. "Positive thoughts!"

I am positive our principal has no idea what she is talking about.

The crowd thins quickly once the ambulance pulls away. Mom has to stay and talk to the police, so she tells Noah and me to walk home. Instead, we head to Oscar's house hoping Oscar will be there soon. Several hours later, Noah and I are still waiting on the Villanuevas' front porch. Mom is inside talking with Oscar's parents. Uncle Pete, Mrs. Ballard, and a very tall police officer are in there too. Oscar is still in the hospital.

"Riley," Noah whispers. "This is all my fault."

In the street, a car without headlights cruises past. Otherwise, the neighborhood is dark and cold and quiet.

I rub my hands together and lean toward the Villanuevas' front window to peek inside. Beyond a small front living room, the adults are crowded around a square table in a brightly lit kitchen. I can't tell who's talking or what's happening.

"It's not your fault," I say.

Noah shakes his head. "I should have known Oscar was upset about the Day of the Dead stuff."

"It's not your fault," I say again.

"And then he rushed out of the classroom. And then he ran in front of your mother's car." Noah sighs. "We should have been looking out for him."

At least we can agree about that.

"My mom and I were arguing about a stupid song on the radio," I tell Noah. "I was playing with the volume and totally distracting her, and—"

"And that's when you hit him?"

I nod.

The two of us sit without speaking for a long moment.

"What song was it?" Noah finally asks.

"Excuse me?"

"You said you were arguing about a song."

"Something about a mule. There was yodeling involved. I wanted to turn it down, but my mom wouldn't let me."

"Yodeling?"

"*Yodel-a-ee . . . He-he-he-he-he-he.* My mother was singing along at the top of her lungs. It was embarrassing."

" 'Mule Skinner Blues,' " Noah says seriously.

"Mule what?"

"It's the Mighty Mighty Mules' fight song. Dolly Parton sings it. You're supposed to play it loud."

"Because of school spirit?" I ask.

"Because of Dolly Parton."

I turn to face Noah. "Because of Dolly Parton, we almost killed Oscar Villanueva."

"Do not blame Dolly Parton," Noah tells me. "Dolly Parton is a powerful force for good in the world."

"I thought that was donuts."

Before Noah can defend donuts or Dolly Parton, the Villanuevas' front door swings open. Mom follows the tall policeman onto the porch. Inside, Uncle Pete and Mrs. Ballard are still at the kitchen table with Oscar's parents. The Villanuevas are both crying.

"Are they okay?" I ask.

"It's been a long day," says Mom.

The police officer, whose badge says his last name is Scott, turns to Mom. "Call me if you need anything, Suze."

Mom nods. "Thanks, Scotty."

"Suze?" I say when the policeman is out of earshot. "Scotty?"

Mom makes a face at me. "He eats at the diner."

"Of course he does."

"And we went to high school together."

I consider my mother for a moment and remember that she actually has a history in West Beacon. She can even yodel along with the Mighty Mighty Mules' fight song. Maybe our family tree isn't just a bunch of broken branches after all.

"When will Oscar be home?" Noah asks now.

"Tomorrow or the next day," Mom tells us. "He's going to be on crutches for a while."

"What about football?" I ask.

Mom sighs. "I'm afraid Oscar's football season might be over."

The three of us turn back to the window. In the kitchen, Mrs. Ballard is crying now too.

CHAPTER 18

OSCAR

I am back in school less than a week after the accident. The doctors promise that I am going to be okay. It's even possible that I might play football again this season. That's if the Mules can win a few games without me, if other teams in our league can lose at the exact right time, and if everything goes well with my healing and rehab routines.

"That's a lot of ifs," says Father Pete, who drops by our house to check on me. He's been visiting at least once a week since Carmen died. "Try to stay focused on what's important now."

"I'm doing all the exercises the doctors gave me," I tell him.

"Have you apologized to your art teacher?"

"He did," says Mom, who's with us at the kitchen table.

I also asked Mr. Martin if I could skip the Día de los Muertos skull assignment. He agreed right away, which makes me think Mrs. James may have reminded him about Carmen. Either way, I appreciate it. Now I hobble across the cafeteria on two crutches. I'm also trying to carry my lunch bag, an overstuffed backpack, a big water bottle, some pens and pencils, and a couple notebooks. It's not going well.

"You could let us help you," Riley suggests as I approach our lunch table.

"I've got this," I tell her. With that, I trip over a chair leg, drop all my things, and fall into Riley's open arms. Luckily, she is stronger than she looks.

Riley shoves me back onto my feet.

"Let me guess," says Noah, who gets my stuff off the floor. "You meant to do that."

"Not so much," I admit.

Noah places everything on the table, then slides a chair behind me. Riley takes my backpack so I can lower myself into the seat. The weight of the bag nearly pulls her arms out of their sockets. "What's in here?" she asks.

"It's just books."

"It feels like a bag of rocks."

"That's because knowledge is worth its weight in gold," says Noah.

Riley rolls her eyes, then takes a seat. I rub my hip, which popped out of its socket during the car accident. I'm not sure if it happened when the car hit me or when I hit the pavement. Either way, putting things back together required strapping me to a hospital bed while a big nurse forced my bones into the right place. I was asleep for that, but I'm still sore now. In the end, except for a bump on my head plus a few scrapes and bruises, the dislocated hip is my only real injury. "You're a very lucky young man," a doctor told me when I woke up. "It could have been a lot worse."

I wonder how bad things have to get before I'm allowed to feel unlucky.

I eat my sandwich, then pull an apple plus a handful of pretzel sticks out of my lunch bag.

"Oscar," Riley says out of the blue. "I distracted my mother while she was driving."

I bite into the apple. "You shouldn't do that."

"That's why she hit you."

I lower the apple. "What?"

"I distracted my mother," Riley says again. "I was playing with the radio. I was being annoying. It was like a TV commercial for exactly what not to do in a car that's driving through a school zone. She probably could have stopped if I wasn't in her face the whole time."

"And then she hit me?"

"It's my fault," says Riley.

"That's not right," Noah says now. "I'm the one who yelled when he was crossing the street. And I'm the one who went on and on about the Day of the Dead even though he didn't want to talk about it." He turns to face me. "I called your name, and you pulled your sweatshirt over your head so you wouldn't have to deal with me. I made you run away."

"You think this is your fault?" I say.

Both Noah and Riley nod at the same time.

"And it had nothing to do with me crossing the street without looking where I was going?"

Around us, the cafeteria hums with laughing and talk and the occasional random crash of trays and books and people tripping and falling over one another.

"That might have had something to do with it," says Noah. "But—"

"But what? It was a really stupid thing to do, and I did it to myself." I point a pretzel stick at Riley and Noah. "Here's a possibility. Maybe it was just an accident."

Riley takes my pretzel. "Whether it was an accident or not, I'm still really sorry."

Noah nods. "Me too."

I rub my hip. "Not as sorry as I am."

Noah glances at my crutches. "I hope we can still be friends."

"We're still friends," I promise.

"In that case," Riley says to me, "you should apologize."

That's unexpected. "For what?"

She pops the pretzel into her mouth. "Your poor decision-making made Noah and me believe we'd nearly committed murder."

"She's right about that," says Noah.

"That's some serious mental anguish and emotional distress for both of us." Riley turns to Noah. "We could probably sue him for millions and trillions of dollars."

"Each," says Noah. "Or Oscar could just let us help him carry his things until he is off the crutches."

"But not his backpack," says Riley. "That's too heavy."

"I'm the one who got hit by the car," I remind them. "Am I really supposed to feel bad about hurting your feelings?"

"You really are," Riley tells me.

"In that case, I am very sorry about the serious mental anguish and emotional distress that happened to you because I got run over by your car."

"And you will accept our help," says Noah.

"And I will accept your help," I agree.

"Congratulations," says Riley. "You just saved yourself millions and trillions of dollars."

"Thank you."

Noah grins. "That's what friends are for."

Even with help, I am exhausted by the end of the school day. At home, I'm too tired and sore to concentrate on my homework so I sit and stare at a chessboard I set up on the kitchen table. The game is the one that used to be in Carmen's hospital room. I have a perfectly good chess set with no missing pieces under my bed, but I stole this one anyway. It feels like a prize I won in a stupid carnival game. It's junky and cheap, but I want to keep it forever.

My parents are still at work, so my opponent is a giant stuffed ibis named Sebastian. The bird is a mascot sent from one of the college football teams that's trying to recruit me.

"Your move," I tell Sebastian, who is playing the white pieces.

The ibis just sits there and stares at me with a big, stupid expression on his beak.

"Fine." I reach over and bring his king's pawn to a center square.

I have to be careful because the board, which is supposed to be a battlefield, is lumpy and creased. Also, our soldiers, at least the ones that aren't missing, are lightweight and plastic, so they tip easily.

I lift my own king's pawn and move it forward one space.

A good thing about getting run over by a car, assuming you don't get killed or injured too badly, is that you get time to think about stuff. I've been thinking about chess pieces because I still want to make my own set. Since the accident, I've learned that standard-looking chess pieces like the ones I'm playing with now were inspired by ancient Greek and Roman artwork and architecture. Unfortunately, the chessmen I've attempted so far look less like Corinthian columns and more like microwaved marshmallow Peeps.

I let Sebastian bring out his queen's pawn.

"You are so predictable," I say, and respond with my own black queen's pawn.

While Sebastian considers his next move, I notice a small notecard attached to one of the stuffed bird's hands. I take a closer look and see that the university president has written me a personal note. He wants me to know that ancient Egyptians considered the ibis a god of wisdom, writing, science, and art, and that I can have all those things myself if I play football for Sebastian's school. I'm sorry, but there's no way Carmen would ever let me play football at a school that sends notes pinned to a stuffed bird's hand. I can hear her now. "Oscar, birds don't even have hands!"

Speaking of football, I really should have gone to practice today, but spending two hours standing on the sidelines would have been torture. In addition to making me feel useless, I'd have been forced to pretend that my hip doesn't hurt. In truth, I feel like somebody is pounding a hot nail into my side.

Sebastian surprises me by taking my pawn. I go ahead and take one of his pawns too. He replies with his king's bishop, so I use a jelly bean to do the same thing on my side of the board. Pretty soon, the bird and I've got knights hopping, jelly beans jumping, and pawns dying. We've both castled, and the plush ibis has just found himself on the wrong side of an unbalanced position.

"You're going down," I warn the mascot.

It's true. I know exactly how to beat my little feathered friend. There's only one problem: I hate this dumb bird, I miss my sister, and I am not having fun.

I know that's more than one problem, and that makes me even more unhappy.

I grab the stuffed toy by the neck and yank him out of his seat. One of his foam feet catches the edge of the chessboard and flips the pieces into the air. Kings, queens, pawns, and bishops crash to the floor.

"Now you've done it," I say.

I grab my crutches, then bring Sebastian outside. I carry him to the side of the house where we keep the trash. A moment later, I shove the bird into a garbage can. Earth to earth, dust to dust, and mascot to basket. I slam the lid and smack the metal can with my crutch.

"That's where you belong."

Back in the kitchen, I sit on the floor to collect the chess pieces. In addition to a lost bishop and absent pawns, the black knight seems to have gone missing now too. I slide across the linoleum and look under the table. While I'm down there, I happen to glance up. That's when I see the fading artwork scrawled on the table's underside.

At first, I laugh out loud because I know exactly what I've discovered. When Carmen was in preschool, she went through a drawing-on-everything stage. Our parents wanted to kill her. I don't remember if they ever caught her in the act. She was as quick as a professional graffiti artist. Somehow, she made art everywhere—walls, shoes, computer screens, and once, on the inside of a toilet. Rather than use crayons and pencils, Carmen preferred a set of brightly colored permanent markers, which she hid in the house like a squirrel protecting its walnuts. Those markers are probably still around here somewhere.

Staring at her work now, I really can't blame my parents for being upset. Carmen really was not a very good artist. Just the same, I am overwhelmed by emotion. And isn't that what art is supposed to do? To make us feel something? If so, this is a masterpiece.

I stare at a dark orange swirl, which I assume is the sun. It floats above a blue line that must be the ocean. Looking more closely, I see a stick figure girl standing in the water. Her grin is bigger than her face, so that's a little weird. Still, it looks just like Carmen. And no surprise, she's talking. It takes a moment for me to decipher the blocky green letters printed above her head.

Hi Oscar. Tell me when you find this. I love you!
From,
Carmen

I lie on my back and read the line over and over again. Finally, I close my eyes, and I wonder if there will ever be a time when I am not broken.

CHAPTER 19

NOAH

It's lunchtime, but Oscar and I are seated at pottery wheels near the back of Mr. Martin's classroom. A light dusting of cold snow covers the grounds outside, but inside, the art room is as hot as a pizza oven. "You're really good at this," says Riley, who is standing behind Oscar and me while we work.

"He's a natural," Mr. Martin agrees.

I nod. "It just takes practice."

"Noah," says Riley. "We're not talking about you."

I look up from my work. "What?"

Mr. Martin leans toward Oscar's wheel, where a ball of wet clay is slowly but surely turning into a shallow, well-shaped bowl. "If the football thing doesn't work out, you might have a future in pottery."

Oscar doesn't look up. "The football thing is going to work out."

Mr. Martin sips coffee from a black mug shaped like an upside-down top hat. "In case it doesn't."

"It will."

I watch Oscar, who is using his thumb and fingers to shape the rim on his bowl. It's hard to believe this is the first time he's ever used the pottery wheel.

"Did you know you wanted it to look like that when you started?" Riley asks him.

Oscar stays focused on his piece. "I kind of let the clay tell me what it wanted to be."

"Why doesn't my clay talk to me?"

"Maybe it does, and you're not listening," I tell her.

She nods. "I think it's telling me to be an accountant."

Mr. Martin laughs. "The world needs accountants too, Riley."

I add some water to the clay on my wheel. The moisture with the smooth earth makes a smell like rain. Mr. Martin points at the onion-shaped vase forming beneath my hands. "You're just showing off, Noah."

I smile because Mr. Martin is right. I glance at Oscar. "You have to admit that this is more fun than football."

Oscar lets his wheel come to a stop. "Football is a different kind of fun."

"Making things is better than breaking things."

"You never want to break things?" Riley asks me.

"Not for fun," I tell her.

Mr. Martin steps forward and helps Oscar remove his finished bowl from the wheel.

"Can I start making chess pieces now?" Oscar asks.

Mr. Martin puts the bowl aside. "Not yet."

Oscar looks a little annoyed. "Why not?"

"First make two good matching bowls. Then you can try to make thirty-two matching chess pieces."

"How do I learn to make two good matching bowls?"

"Noah?" says Mr. Martin.

I laugh. "First you make ten thousand that don't match."

"Ten thousand?" says Oscar.

I point at the really nice bowl Oscar just finished. "One down."

"Making one quality piece is hard," says Mr. Martin. "Doing it again and again and again is even harder, but that's what it means to be good at something."

Mr. Martin might not be the best teacher in the world, but he does know what he's talking about. Also, it's really nice of him to let us start our own little clay club during his lunch break.

A bell rings to announce the end of the period, so Mr. Martin heads to his desk to get ready for the next class. With Riley's help, Oscar and I clean up our wheels and workspace. I move Oscar's bowl and my vase to a drying rack, where I notice another one of Riley's attempts at a clay football. This one resembles a giant walnut.

"It's not good," Riley says from behind me.

"No," I admit. "Not really."

Leaving his crutches behind, Oscar hops across the room to join us. He points at Riley's sculpture. "Is that a brain?"

Riley crosses her arms.

"Don't be mad," I tell her. "You're getting better."

"Not as good as either one of you."

"I can't make a brain," says Oscar.

Riley sighs. "At least you have a brain."

"What are you talking about?" I ask.

"You two are good at everything," she blurts out.

"I can't find my way to the cafeteria," I remind her.

"You're probably getting straight A's in every class, and colleges are already calling Oscar. I can't make a ball out of Play-Doh, and my highest grade is a B because Mr. Martin only gives A's, B's, and F's."

"I promise that I fail at stuff every day."

"Like what?" Riley asks.

"You can fail clay?" says Oscar, who's looking a little wobbly on his feet.

I cross the room and return with a crutch for Oscar, who tucks it beneath one arm.

"Like what?" Riley says again.

I shift uncomfortably, then lower my voice. "My dad basically ran away from home. My mom is still a mess. I'm trying to help, but it's not working. She barely even talks to me."

Oscar leans on his crutch. "Maybe your mom doesn't want to talk about it."

"Maybe I do," I say.

Oscar nods thoughtfully. "Since my sister died, my

whole family is a mess. I'm not really helping either. I'm probably making things worse."

"How could you make things worse?" says Riley.

"My parents want me to share my feelings." Oscar shoots me a look. "I don't want to talk about it."

"Why not?" I ask.

"I know they're hurting. They know I'm hurting. What else is there to say? Plus, it's all too big. We probably wouldn't be able to say what we mean anyway, so I'd rather just keep it to myself. Now my parents think I'm falling apart."

"Are you falling apart?" says Riley.

Oscar glances at his injured leg. "Maybe a little."

"Maybe we're all falling apart a little."

"That's probably why we're friends," says Oscar.

"No," I say. "That's not it."

"What is it, then?" asks Riley.

I have no idea how or why I know the answer to her question, but I am absolutely sure that I am right. "It's because we deserve each other."

CHAPTER 20

OSCAR

After more than two weeks, I'm still in a brace that stretches from my hip to my ankle. The pain hasn't improved, but I'm down to one crutch, and I'm doing upper body work in the weight room every other day. In the meantime, the Mules have won three games in a row, including last night's surprise victory over the Shepton Huskies. We still have a shot at the playoffs, which means I still have a chance to play football again this year.

Today, however, is not a football day. Instead, I am going to Noah's house because Riley and I promised to help Noah with his mother's online pottery store.

"Where is this store located?" Riley asked on Friday during our lunch period.

"It's called the Internet," Noah told her.

Riley wadded up a napkin and threw it at him. "I mean in the real world."

"We run it out of our garage," he explained.

"Is an online pottery store a full-time job?" I asked.

Noah peeled a sorry-looking banana. "It's our family business."

Riley took a big bite of chocolate cake that her mom brought home from the Beacon Diner. "And you make money at it?"

"Sure," he said. "Except for when we don't throw pots, make sales, or fill orders."

"How's it going lately?" I asked.

"Not great. Can you come over tomorrow?"

Thankfully, Riley offered to give me a ride so I don't have to walk. Noah's house is less than a mile away, but hobbling there on one crutch would probably kill me. Even sliding into the back of Father Pete's station wagon makes me gasp.

"Are you okay?" Riley asks as I pull the car door closed.

I nod. "Thanks for the ride."

"Thank my uncle Pete," says Riley. "I forgot my mom was working the breakfast shift, so he came to the rescue."

"It's no problem," says Father Pete, who's wearing his Mighty Mighty Mules letter jacket. "Saving people is sort of my job."

I try to get comfortable, but my hip feels like it's filled with broken glass this morning. Coach Moyer has very specific rules about situations like this. He says, A BENT NAIL SHOULD SPEAK UP BEFORE THE HAMMER COMES DOWN. In other words, we're supposed to report all injuries so we don't get hurt even more. But I know what happens to bent nails. At best, they remain unused. At worst, they get thrown away, so I keep the pain to myself.

I look around the inside of Father Pete's car. It's a big old brown-and-green thing called a Country Squire. It looks like a vehicle the Brady Bunch might have thrown away. "Is this what priests have to drive?"

"The wagon came with the parish," Father Pete explains. "If it was up to me, I'd be driving a red El Camino with flames painted on the side plus a big block Chevy, dual carbs, and a supercharger sticking out of the hood."

"You like cars?" I ask.

"I am a car guy," Father Pete admits. "Sadly, I don't have time to work on them anymore."

"My dad and I want to turn an old pickup truck into a hot rod one day."

"Call me when you're ready," says Father Pete. "I know how to weld, I'm good with engines, and I'll throw in a blessing for free."

After a few quick lefts and rights, we turn up a steep hill and then stop in front of a house with an even steeper driveway. "This old wagon is not going to climb that cliff," the priest tells us.

"We can make it from here," says Riley.

"Thanks again," I tell Father Pete, then step outside.

Once the station wagon pulls away, Riley and I head

toward Noah's house. Unfortunately, my crutch slips on a patch of gravel, and all my weight shifts onto my injured side. The pain makes my knees buckle. Riley tries to catch me, but the driveway's too steep. When I fall, I take us both down. Noah finds us a few moments later sitting on the grass on his front lawn.

"Are you okay?" he asks.

"Never better," says Riley.

"Would you like to come inside?"

Riley gets to her feet. "That sounds very nice."

"Oscar?" says Noah.

I take a deep breath. "I need help."

"We've got you," Noah promises.

It takes all three of us plus the crutch to get me back to a standing position.

"Thank you," I say.

"You'd do the same for us," says Noah.

Riley laughs. "With just one hand."

The three of us, more carefully this time, make our way up the driveway. I don't even try to hide my limp. "Should you still be on two crutches?" Riley asks.

I shake my head. "I have to get back on my feet."

"If you say so."

At the top of the driveway, Noah lifts a big garage door to reveal an indoor space that's been turned into an art studio. It's a lot like the one at school, with pottery wheels and worktables around the room, shelves filled with half-finished pottery along the walls, and old cans and jars holding tools and brushes. A low, squat pug mill sits in one corner of the garage, and two shiny metal kilns sit in the other.

"You have a pottery studio inside your house?" I say.

I never imagined that there were people committed to making art in the same way that you could commit to football, or cooking, or cars.

"My mom and dad put it together right after they got married," says Noah. "Rather than going on a honeymoon, they built a pottery studio. They used to make things all week long and sell them at craft fairs on the weekends. We do most of our business online now."

I remember that Noah's parents are getting a divorce. Riley must be thinking the same thing. "We?" she asks.

"Me and my mom. My dad liked the idea of being a potter more than he liked actually making pots. We sort of fired him."

Riley steps into the studio and examines a green glazed bowl placed at the center of a worktable. "Was that before or after your parents split up?"

Noah considers the question. "I honestly don't know," he finally says.

I point at a huge blue kidney-shaped stain that's spread halfway across the garage floor. "What happened here?"

"I spilled a whole bucket of cerulean-blue glaze," Noah

explains. "It's a long story. It happened a while ago, but that stain might never come out."

Just then, a door that must connect the garage to the kitchen opens. A gray-haired woman in a baseball cap wanders in. I assume it's Noah's mom. She's wearing a wrinkled blue robe over a faded red sweatshirt, loose brown work pants, and a pair of sneakers that might have been white once. Now they're stained with dripped paint and pottery glaze. Without greeting us, she shuffles across the garage to the back wall, where she opens an old white refrigerator and pulls out two glass bottles of orange soda.

"Help yourself," she tells us, then returns to the kitchen.

"That was my mother," Noah says once the kitchen door is closed. It's clear that he's a little embarrassed.

"Is she okay?" Riley asks.

He shrugs. "This week has been better than last week."

I have a feeling there is more to Noah's parents' divorce than pottery. I guess it must be bad, but you'd never know it from Noah. Of course, you'd never know what's been going on at my house from looking at my own mother, who is up and dressed and ready for work every single day. Not only that, she makes sure Dad and I are on track and moving forward full speed ahead too. Inside, I don't think any of us are any less broken than Noah's mom appears to be. I guess everybody falls apart and holds it together—or not—in their own way.

"Where do you want us to start?" I ask Noah.

"Mugs are top sellers during the holidays. I thought we'd make some."

"Sure," I say.

"I hate to break this to you," says Riley. "But nobody is going to pay for anything I make."

Noah nods. "That's true."

Riley shoots Noah a dirty look. "You didn't have to agree so fast."

"Don't worry," he says. "I already figured out a way for you to help."

A moment later, Noah's got Riley set up at a table with a fat slab of clay, a rolling pin, and a set of metal cookie cutters including leaves, stars, hearts, little musical instruments, and different sports shapes too. "Roll out a flat sheet about a quarter-inch thick. After that, use the cookie cutters to make clay shapes."

"I can do that," says Riley.

"Later, we'll add handles and attach the shapes so that every mug is sort of unique. Then we'll fire them, glaze them, fire them again, and photograph the finished pieces to sell online."

"We're going to do all that today?" says Riley.

Noah shakes his head. "Between the making and the drying and the decorating and the glazing and then the kiln, and assuming nothing cracks or chips or explodes, we'll have finished mugs in about a week."

"This is a lot of work for a cup," says Riley.

"That's why I'm glad you're here." Noah pulls a few cookie cutters aside. "People like hearts, stars, and sports shapes the best."

"Then that's what I'll make," Riley promises.

I follow Noah to the other side of the garage. He points me to a low stool in front of a well-used pottery wheel. I shove my crutch out of the way and drop into the seat. It feels good to sit down. "Now what?" I ask.

Noah shows me a pile of apple-sized balls made out of a dull gray clay. "I prepared these ahead of time."

"How many?" I ask.

He takes a seat at a nearby wheel. "Forty. That's how many mugs will fit into our kiln." He grabs a clay apple and flings it straight down onto the center of his wheel. It makes a loud *splat!*

"Do you really have to throw it that hard?"

"You don't have to, but it's more fun if you do."

I smile, grab a ball of clay, and then throw it down onto my wheel. I dip my hands into a plastic container filled with water and then center my piece just like Mr. Martin showed me in class. I also watch Noah because he's a lot better at this than I am. "Any advice?" I ask.

Noah places the heel of his left hand on top of the spinning ball and then braces his right hand against the left. "When you're centering, remember that your hands move the clay. Not the other way around." He presses down on a foot pedal, and the pottery wheel begins to spin. In just a couple seconds, he guides the lump beneath his hands into the shape of a perfect, spinning cylinder. "Now I can work with it."

"That's amazing."

"I haven't made anything yet," he points out.

"It's still amazing."

Pushing down, Noah turns the cylinder into a wide flat disc. Using both hands, he shapes the spinning clay into a cone. Now he flattens and rounds the clay into something like a fat hockey puck. With a thumb and a couple fingers, he pushes down and creates a hole in the puck's center. The opening widens quickly. Noah lifts the sides so that it's more of a cylinder again, except now it's hollow.

"It's a mug!" I say.

"Not quite." Noah takes a small metal scraper from the workbench and runs the flat edge against the outside of his spinning piece. With the lightest touch, he peels clay away and gives the outside of the mug a gentle, curved shape. Finally, he runs a small wet sponge around the top to create a neat round lip. "Now it's a mug."

"Except for drying and glazing and a handle and the kiln and Riley's decorations and possibly exploding."

"Not in that order, but yes," Noah agrees.

"It's a lot of work for a cup!" Riley hollers from across the room.

"It's worth it," Noah calls back.

"Can I have one when we're done?" she says.

Noah laughs. "What do you think you're getting for Christmas?"

"How much does a finished mug cost?" I ask.

Noah slides a wire beneath the piece to separate his clay from the pottery wheel. "Around fifty dollars."

Now I understand how an online pottery store could be a real job. Still, you'd need to sell a lot of mugs to make a living at this.

"Fifty dollars for a cup?" says Riley.

"It's art." Noah moves the mug to a drying rack. "And it's a really nice cup."

"I've changed my mind," Riley announces. "I don't want one for Christmas. I'd be afraid to drink out of it."

"You don't think you're worth fifty dollars?" Noah asks.

"I'm worth a lot more than that, but nobody is worth a fifty-dollar cup."

"Just for that, you're getting the mug, a flowerpot, and a set of soup bowls too." Noah turns and points at the ball of clay on my wheel. "You try, Oscar."

I stare at my pottery wheel for a moment. It really is a very simple thing. It looks like an old-fashioned record player sitting inside a shallow plastic bucket. I close my eyes for a moment and think of all the steps that Noah just made.

"It's kind of like a conversation," Noah says now.

My eyes pop open. "What?"

"In class you said you listen to what the clay wants to be," Noah reminds me. "That's great for just one bowl, but when you're making a whole bunch of identical pieces, you have to find a way to make the clay listen to you too."

"What if it doesn't?" I ask.

"The clay hardly ever listens to you, and the pieces almost never come out the way they look in your head. You have to sort of work together to figure out something that's good enough for both of you to live with."

I lean forward, cup my hand around the clay ball, and start my wheel. Slowly, I'm able to turn the ball into a cylinder, then a cone, and then a puck. From there, I use my fingers to re-form the shape, and suddenly I've got a tube-shaped cup. After some pinching and scraping, I have an actual mug. "I did it!"

Noah leans over and gives me a high five.

"You guys are weird," Riley says from her side of the room.

Neither Noah nor I tell Riley that she's been singing "Three Blind Mice" under her breath for the last ten minutes. I've noticed that she likes to sing little nursery rhymes when she gets focused on her work. I don't think she even knows she's doing it.

"You fit right in," Noah calls back.

I use a wire to slice the first mug off my wheel. I put the piece aside and then grab another ball of clay. Before

I begin again, I look up and catch the expression on my friends' faces. Like me, they're grinning from ear to ear. I know exactly why. It's because we are making things together. It's because we are a good team.

"If you come over again, we can finish this batch and start another one," says Noah.

"Sure," says Riley.

"Count me in." I hesitate a moment, then ask a question. "Can I invite you to something too?"

Riley looks my way. She's holding the rolling pin in one hand as if she's about to chase somebody down and whack them in the head. "What is it?"

"Father Pete is going to say a Mass for my sister. Would you like to come?"

She nods. "I can do that."

"Me too." Noah moves my first piece to a nearby drying rack. I can't help but notice that it looks just as good as the other mugs on the shelf. It looks like it belongs.

"Mass is on Monday," I say. "It's at six thirty."

"At night?" Riley asks hopefully.

"In the morning."

"We'll be there," Noah says.

"In the morning?" Riley looks like she's in shock.

"She'll be there," Noah tells me.

"Of course I'll be there." Riley throws a pea-sized ball of clay at Noah's head. "I might be walking in my sleep, but I'll be there."

Noah ducks, and we all laugh. I want to say thank you, but suddenly I can't speak because I have been struck by a sudden and terrible thought. Carmen will never ever know my friends, and they will never really know her.

CHAPTER 21

RILEY

Early Monday morning, Mom and I stand alone inside Saint Barbara's Church. "Riley," Mom says. "Where is everybody?"

I stop in the doorway that leads into the main part of the building. "I guess we're early."

Mom walks halfway down the center aisle. She stops and then starts spinning in a slow circle to look all around. "Everything is exactly the same."

I told her about the early morning Mass after supper last night. She surprised me by offering to come along because, in her words, "Oscar must be a very special friend."

"Why do you say that?" I asked.

"Because he's still talking to you even after we almost ran him over."

"We didn't *almost* run him over," I pointed out.

Now Mom and I stare at the church's painted ceiling and the stained glass that glows in the early morning sunlight.

"What's exactly the same?" I ask.

Mom stops turning. She places a hand on a worn wooden bench. "This place. It hasn't changed a bit." She breathes deeply. "It even smells the same."

"It smells like burnt marshmallows."

"That's incense," Mom tells me.

"What's incense?"

"It's—" She stops. "I don't actually know."

"Is it made out of burnt marshmallows?"

"No."

Mom slides onto one of the wooden benches. I join her, and we sit quietly for a moment. Mom glances at her watch. "It's six thirty-five, Riley. Are you sure you got the time right?"

"I'm sure."

"And the day?"

"I know what day it is."

"Maybe it's next Monday?"

"We are in the right place on the right day at the right time." I guess I'm speaking a lot louder than necessary, because my voice echoes inside the big open church building.

"You don't need to shout," Mom whispers.

"Sorry."

"We'll give them a few more minutes."

We sit without speaking for about sixty seconds. I know because I'm counting. Finally, I turn to my mother, who's got her eyes closed. "Should we say a prayer or something?"

"Riley," she says, "the highest form of prayer is to stand silently in awe before God."

"Where did that come from?" I ask.

Mom, eyes still shut, grins. "It's on a plaque next to the cash register at that Lebanese takeout place you like in Philly."

I don't remember the plaque, but I definitely remember the manakeesh, which is sort of like a Lebanese pizza. There is no manakeesh in West Beacon.

"Do you miss Philadelphia?" Mom asks out of the blue.

In Philadelphia, my school cafeteria was probably big enough to hold the entire town of West Beacon. Despite that, I didn't have many friends. I always felt overwhelmed by the crushes and the heartbreaks and the spitballs and just the nonstop drama and chaos that came with a building filled with a thousand sixth, seventh, and eighth graders. "No," I say. "But . . ."

"But what?"

"I wish we didn't run away."

"Run away?" says Mom.

"After you saw the man with the gun, you just packed us up, and we ran away from Philadelphia."

"That's what you think?"

"That's what happened."

Mom, eyes open now, stares at the front of the church for a long time. Finally, she says, "Can I tell you a story?"

I nod. "Okay."

"Once upon a time, a lady came out of a grocery store, and a man tried to steal one of her bags. The two of them ended up in a tug of war, and it didn't take long for the bag, which was filled with apples, to rip. The apples dropped and started rolling around on the ground. The man raced after the apples. He picked up as many as he could, and then he ran away. That's when the lady realized that the man was hungry. Later, she visited her priest and told him what happened. She said, 'Father, I try to be a good person, but today I literally snatched food out of the hands of a hungry person. What could I have done differently?'

" 'Did you happen to buy any soda at the grocery store?' the priest asked her.

" 'I did,' said the lady.

" 'You should have taken the biggest bottle of soda, shaken it up, and then opened it in the man's face,' the priest told her. 'Maybe blasting him with soda pop would have opened his eyes to the fact that he is on the wrong path.' "

I turn to my mother. "That's the story?"

She nods. "That's the story."

"Is it a true story?"

"No," Mom says. "In real life you should give the groceries to the robber so nobody gets hurt."

"So it's okay that I didn't spray soda at the man with the gun?"

"Riley," says Mom. "I think the man with the gun sprayed soda in my face."

"I was there," I remind her. "He put a gun in your face."

"And that was really scary," she says. "But my point is that I needed to wake up. I needed to have my eyes opened to the fact that I was on the wrong path. I did nothing but work all the time because everything was so expensive in the city. That meant I hardly got to be with you. I spent most of my time with strangers. I was lonely and worried and—"

"Cranky?"

"That's not what I was going to say."

"Sorry."

"And by the way, that wasn't the first time I got robbed at the cash register."

My mouth drops open. "That wasn't the first time?"

She ignores me and keeps talking. "I still love Philadelphia, but I wasn't able to make a good home for us there. I should have seen that a while ago. I needed something to make me realize that it was past time for a change. Maybe the man with the gun inspired me to open my eyes."

"So the man with the gun is supposed to be the lady with the groceries," I say slowly. "Are you the one who was trying to steal the apples? And who's the priest?"

"Forget the story, Riley."

"I don't even know what the story is," I tell her.

Mom laughs, then points at the statue of Saint Stephen. "Do you know the story of the Holy Dexter?"

"I've heard of it," I admit.

"When I was in seventh grade, I got in trouble for handing in a paper that referred to Saint Stephen as Jesus's right-hand man."

"That sounds like something Uncle Pete would say."

"That's because he did say it. He wrote the paper for me."

"You cheated?"

Mom shrugs.

"Did Uncle Pete get in trouble too?"

"I am not a snitch."

"You cheated and you lied?"

"And now your uncle is a priest, which proves, once again, that God has a sense of humor."

I look around at the artwork and sculptures that fill the church. "Why did Uncle Pete become a priest anyway?"

Mom is quiet for a long time.

"Is it a secret?" I ask.

She shakes her head. "Your uncle and I did not grow up in a happy family."

Mom hardly ever talks about her parents, so I say nothing in hopes that she will go on.

"Your grandparents were hard people," she finally continues. "It seemed like they wanted your uncle and me to be that way too."

"Why?"

"They always felt as if a lot had been taken away from them. They moved to West Beacon from Centralia, which is not very far from here. That's where they grew up. It's where they expected to live and work and die. It was their town, and they thought it would never change. But then an underground fire in the coal mines spread beneath most of Centralia. People lost their homes, and everybody had to leave. Your grandparents spent the rest of their lives angry about it."

"It sounds like they had a reason to be angry."

"You can always find a reason to be angry, Riley."

"What does this have to do with being a priest?"

"When we moved to West Beacon, there was an old Hungarian pastor named Father Kovacs. He had a big laugh, and he always made you feel like the world was better because you were in it. He used to come to school at recess and teach us all how to catch and throw a football, which, in case you haven't figured it out, is also a religion around here."

"You played football?"

"Your uncle had to play catch with somebody."

"So Uncle Pete is a priest because an old Hungarian man showed you both how to play football?"

"I think your uncle Pete always wanted to be someone who could laugh and be kind and be good in the world. Father Kovacs showed him a way to make that happen."

I think about this, then ask another question. "Why did you stop going to church?"

Mom looks up and around at the small pretty space where we're sitting. "Lots of reasons," she finally says. "Some of them even make sense."

"Do you think you'll ever go back?"

"I'm here now, aren't I?" She looks at her watch again. "Riley, we are either in the right place at the wrong time or the wrong place at the right time. Which is it?"

"The time is right," I insist. "Where else—"

Suddenly, Mom gets to her feet. "The chapel!"

"The what?"

She grabs my arm and pulls me off the bench. "Come on!"

Before I can protest, Mom drags me down the aisle and toward the altar. At the last minute, she drops to one knee, bows her head, and touches a finger to her forehead.

"What are you doing?"

"Genuflect!" she tells me.

"Genu-what?"

She sighs. "You really don't know any of this."

"How would I—"

Mom doesn't give me time to finish. She pulls me outside, where we rush down a sidewalk leading toward the back of the church. A moment later, we stop in front of a small wooden door that looks like the entrance to an underground tomb. "What's in there?"

"Follow me," says Mom. "We'll apologize later."

"For what?"

Mom doesn't answer. She just pushes the door open and drags me inside. It's a small space, less than half the size of one of our classrooms at school. It smells like a combination of wet dog and carpet cleaner. Uncle Pete, wearing his green robes, stands at a table before a small group all seated on metal folding chairs. Oscar is in the front row with his parents. Noah's squeezed into a back corner with his mom. Mrs. Wright's got her hair pulled back into a thick ponytail today. She looks better than the last time I saw her. A couple men and women are dressed for work, but the rest of the crowd is mostly older people in sweaters and comfortable shoes. Mom and I find two empty chairs at the end of one row. A few seats away, a little old lady dressed in bright pink sweatpants and a matching top sits between us and the wall. She gives me a quick smile. "Better late than never," she whispers.

At the front of the room, Uncle Pete lifts something that looks like a tortilla over his head. About half the crowd kneels on the floor. For some, the kneeling is obviously difficult and even painful, but they don't seem to mind. A couple minutes later, Uncle Pete invites everyone to line up and accept a piece of bread. Noah had me skip this part last time, but I watched the routine, and I think I know what to do now. I go to stand, but Mom stops me. "Not us," she whispers.

"Why not?"

"You're not ready, and I'd probably get struck by lightning."

"I didn't eat breakfast!" I remind her.

Mom smiles a little. "It's not that kind of bread."

I have no idea what she's talking about, but I still stay seated. Meanwhile, everybody else heads for the front of the room except for me and Mom. The old woman in pink leans toward us and whispers loudly, "You're blocking my way."

"Sorry." Mom and I stand so she can get by.

The woman struggles to her feet with the help of a cane. Very slowly, she makes her way to Uncle Pete, accepts a piece of bread, and then returns to the chair next to mine. After a quiet moment, she leans forward and whispers in my ear. "See those people in the front row?" She points at Oscar's parents and continues talking before I can reply. "We need to pray for them. This Mass is for their little girl. She died."

"I—"

The old lady cuts me off. "You think you'll never get over something like that. In a lot of ways, you never do. Then one day you realize that the last tragedy was getting you ready for the next one. If you're lucky, you end up thankful for it all."

I lean back and speak a little more harshly than I probably should. "Nobody should be thankful for that."

"Is that what you think?" she asks.
"That's what I think," I tell her.
She smiles. "Then I will pray for you too."

CHAPTER 22

OSCAR

Mrs. Baptiste is prettier than I remember. Of course, I was crumpled beneath her front bumper the last time we met. All I saw then was a couple skinny ankles connected to a pair of black sneakers with pink laces. I glance down and realize that Riley and her mother wear the exact same shoes. I wonder if Riley knows that she's basically a smaller version of her mom.

"How's the leg?" Mrs. Baptiste asks me once we leave the chapel. Outside, we stand in the cool morning shadow of Saint Barbara's church.

"I'm off the crutches," I tell her.

"You are?" says Noah, who's joined us.

I saw him with his mother during Mass, but Mrs. Wright is gone now. I guess she doesn't like crowds. I lift my arms up from my sides. "Today's my first day."

It's true. I've convinced my parents—and myself—that I can walk on my own. It's also true that lightning bolts of pain shoot through my hip when I move, but that was true when I was on crutches too. I figure I'm going to hurt no matter what I do, so I might as well get back on my feet and back on track with football.

"I'm really sorry," Mrs. Baptiste says now.

"It was an accident," my mom offers, as if she doesn't want to kill everybody for all the bad things that have happened to her children during the last few months.

"I'm also very sorry about your daughter," Mrs. Baptiste adds.

Mom nods. "Carmen was a good girl."

It's weird how a single word can make so many things happen at once. Hearing my sister's name makes my ears ring and my eyes burn. My father shoves both hands into his pockets and lowers his head. It actually feels like the world tilts on its axis a little bit.

Mrs. Baptiste takes a deep breath. "I can't imagine what this has been like. I still feel terrible about hurting Oscar. I am so sorry."

Suddenly, my mother is crying. Riley's mother is crying too. Now the two of them are standing in the grass and hugging. Finally, Mrs. Baptiste takes a step back. She uses a sleeve to rub her nose. "I'm glad we got that out of the way."

"I know." Mom sniffs and laughs a little.

Mrs. Baptiste offers a sad smile. "You really wanted to kill me."

Mom nods. "I really did."

They laugh together. I look to my father, who shrugs. I'm glad I'm not the only one who doesn't get the joke.

"I'm sorry we were late," Mrs. Baptiste says now. "We were sitting all alone in the church."

Riley leans toward me and whispers, "You didn't tell me about the chapel."

"Sorry," I say.

She looks down at my injured leg. "Can you walk to school with us?"

I shake my head. "I'm taking the day off."

"Oscar has a doctor's appointment," Mom explains. "There's one final exam and then back to school after lunch."

"We'll see," I say, because I expect the excitement level to be a little overwhelming once everybody hears that I can play football again. I wouldn't mind spending one more afternoon hiding in my room before I'm back in the middle of the storm.

"You'll probably have practice today," Dad reminds me.

"Then we'll be in the bleachers," says Riley.

"We will?" asks Noah.

Riley nods. "We'll be Oscar's cheering section."

"Try not to embarrass me," I tell them.

"We will be Oscar's understated but very enthusiastic cheering section," says Riley.

"I guess we'll see you soon," says Noah.

There's a sudden breeze, and a deep chill touches my hip and bones. I'd like to start moving, but the sharp cold and the pain in my leg might turn my first step into a noticeable limp. I don't want my parents to see that, so I throw an arm around Noah and put my weight on his shoulder. "Not if I see you first."

Noah staggers back and pulls me away from the church's shadow just as a bright sun appears from behind the cloud. The warmth plus the motion forces me to pivot on my hip and take a first step. Once I make that first move, that first step, I have some flexibility, and I can walk normally again.

"I don't want to sit at the top of the bleachers," Noah tells Riley.

"Why not?" she asks.

"I don't like heights."

"I think today would be a good day to face your fears."

While the two of them bicker and laugh, I stand on my own and take another step. It's not a problem. All I have to do is take a step, ignore the pain, and keep going. Maybe that's the trick to everything.

Step. Ignore. Go.

CHAPTER 23

NOAH

After school, I follow Riley to the top of the practice field bleachers. They are not as high as I expected them to be. At least that's what I keep telling myself. The sun is bright, but it's still the middle of November, so it's cold out here. Today, the Mighty Mighty Mules are practicing in silver-and-brown football helmets plus shoulder pads, but instead of regular uniforms, the players are all wearing sweatpants.

"Where's the extra padding?" I ask.

"The next game isn't until Thanksgiving," Riley explains. "That's more than a week away, so Coach won't make them hit each other every single day till then."

Down below, a player jogging across midfield trips over his own feet and falls flat on his face. "Hitting or not, they should wear Bubble Wrap from head to toe."

Riley laughs. "I'd pay to see that."

"It would be an improvement." I rub my hands together. Down on the field, two boys crash into each other. They fall down, then, just as quickly, get back on their feet again. "We already get plenty of opportunities to hurt one another. I don't understand why people work so hard to invent new ones."

"You can't go through life covered in Bubble Wrap," says Riley.

"Sure you can," I tell her. "That's what friends and family are for."

She turns to me. "Friends and family are Bubble Wrap?"

"The trick is having enough to keep you safe but not so much that you can't breathe."

Riley gives me an odd look. "Do you always think this much about Bubble Wrap?"

"We have a lot of it at the house. It's for packing up pottery. I tried to use it on my parents once, but that didn't work out."

"You tried to pack your parents in Bubble Wrap?"

"I packed myself in Bubble Wrap. My parents were fighting, and I was afraid they were going to hit each other, so I decided to break it up myself. Of course, I wasn't going to do that without some kind of protection."

"You packed yourself in Bubble Wrap?"

"We have a forty-eight-inch-wide roll on a rack in the garage," I explain. "I grabbed one end and spun in a circle until I looked like a big plastic burrito."

Riley stares at me openmouthed.

"It seemed like a good idea at the time."

"And then?"

"The plan was for me to rush into the kitchen and stand between my parents until they both calmed down."

"That didn't work?"

"It might have worked if I hadn't covered my face in Bubble Wrap."

"You couldn't see?" Riley asks.

"I couldn't breathe. Bubble Wrap will totally restrict the oxygen flow going in and out of your body, and don't let anybody tell you different."

Riley starts to laugh.

"I started stumbling around like a giant two-legged banana."

"I thought you were a burrito!"

"Does it really matter?"

She grins. "I guess not."

"Just before I passed out, I tripped and fell onto a rack filled with finished pottery. It tipped and landed on a stack of buckets filled with glaze. One of the buckets actually burst open and spilled all over the garage floor."

"Cerulean blue?" Riley guesses.

"Cerulean blue," I confirm. "When my parents heard all the smashing and crashing, they came running into the garage. I guess they stopped fighting long enough to cut me out of the Bubble Wrap."

"You guess?"

"I don't know for sure because I was unconscious."

Riley is laughing so hard that tears are running down her face. "I'm really glad you didn't die."

"Thanks," I say. "Me too. But in the end, they split up anyway."

"But first they saved your life." Riley wipes her eyes. "And that's not nothing."

"I wish I could have thought of something better to do."

"Something better than packing yourself in Bubble Wrap?" Riley shakes her head. "You can't improve upon perfection."

"I could have cut out a hole for breathing."

"That would have been an improvement," she admits. "But otherwise, I wouldn't change a thing."

The two of us sit and watch football practice without speaking. After a couple minutes, Riley turns to me. "Do you see Oscar?"

I scan the field. "I don't think he's down there."

"He must have stayed home," says Riley. "He wasn't supposed to do that."

"Do you think something's wrong?" I ask.

Riley stands. "I think we should find out."

Together, we make our way across the parking lot and off the school grounds. We cross Lehigh and Market Streets, then head down a slight hill and onto a small road filled with brick and clapboard row houses. Around us, the hills surrounding West Beacon are no longer autumn orange and red. Except for evergreens, the trees are mostly bare branches now. Winter is coming soon.

We make another turn, which brings us to a narrow street filled with more crowded houses. There are no front yards here. Rather, small porches covered by worn awnings look down on a long cracked sidewalk.

"Why does everybody live so close together?" Riley asks.

"The coal company built all these houses for people who came to work in the mines. It's faster and cheaper when you shove everything side by side." I point at a low-slung building that's still home to Kowalonek's Kielbasy Shop. "This was the Polish neighborhood. A couple blocks over was for the Irish. The houses near you were all Hungarian. Different nationalities got put in different sections of town."

"What was the point of that?"

"Keeping everybody apart made it hard for people to organize. When the miners finally started getting together, they were able to demand higher pay and better treatment. When that happened, the coal companies basically declared war on their own workers. Stories about West Beacon from back then make the Wild West sound like Disneyland."

"It sounds like sticking together was dangerous too," says Riley.

"Definitely."

"But sticking together was still the better choice in the long run."

"Isn't that why we're going to find Oscar?" I tell her.

We continue to the next street, where the homes are still packed tight except for a few that sit next to large empty lots that are mostly filled with dry weeds. Crumbling walkways and abandoned foundations reveal that houses once stood on these spaces. I stop and stare at a pile of tumbled-down bricks that probably marks the spot of an old coal stove or maybe a wood fireplace.

Riley points at the bricks. "What happened there?"

"This street is on top of an old section of the coal mine, so—"

"We're on top of the coal mine?"

"Riley," I say. "The whole town is on top of the coal mine. That's why West Beacon got put here in the first place. Anyway, the old shafts flood and collapse sometimes. If there's a house—"

"It falls in?"

"It's more like it tips over."

"So the ground beneath West Beacon can just open up and swallow us?"

"That's not what I'm saying."

"That is exactly what you said."

"Nobody has ever fallen into a hole and not gotten out," I tell her.

Riley looks unhappy. "But people do fall in?"

I shrug. "It happens."

We walk another half block and stop on the sidewalk in front of Oscar's house. Riley and I are both surprised to see that Oscar's actually sitting on his front porch.

Riley raises a hand and waves. "Oscar, where have you been?"

Oscar stands quickly. "I don't want to talk to anybody," he yells at us.

"We're not anybody," Riley tells him.

"Just leave me alone!" Oscar turns, heads into the house, and slams the door shut.

Riley and I exchange a quick look. "Did he just tell us to leave?" she asks.

I nod. "It sounded like that."

"Are we going to leave?"

I shake my head. "Absolutely not."

CHAPTER 24

OSCAR

I was sitting on the front porch because I wanted to be alone. I know this makes no sense, because the house is empty. My parents are both at work. They let me stay home after the doctor gave us the news. Now I'm sitting on the floor inside my own front door while Riley and Noah ring the bell and knock on the windows. I miss the cold air on my face, but I don't go back outside, and I don't answer. I just listen to them call my name.

"Oscar," Riley yells after a long time. "It's getting dark. We have to go soon."

"Then go!" I finally holler back.

"What's wrong?" Noah shouts at me.

"What did we do?" asks Riley.

I sigh. "You didn't do anything."

"Then why are you mad?"

I wish I could say I'm not mad, but I'm a terrible liar. Also, I'm angry enough to explode. Tears run down my face and into my mouth. I taste dirt and salt. "I just don't want to talk to anybody right now."

"Are you crying?" Riley says.

I use a sleeve to wipe my eyes. "No!"

"Please open the door."

"If you don't open the door, we're going to break a window and let ourselves in," says Noah.

That makes me laugh because Noah can barely snap a pretzel in half without worrying about the crumbs. "Just leave me alone."

"Why should we do that?" says Riley.

"Because that's what I want."

There is a long pause, and then Riley speaks again. "I called my uncle Pete. He's on the way."

I put my head in my hands. "Why are you ignoring what I say?"

"That's what friends are for," says Noah.

"We're your Bubble Wrap," adds Riley.

At least that's what I think she said.

Father Pete arrives a few moments later. Thankfully, he forces Riley and Noah into his station wagon and drives them home. Unfortunately, the priest returns quickly. He must have called my parents at work, because they've come home as well. I can't keep Mom and Dad out of their own house, so now we're all sitting around the kitchen table, where I have to relive this day.

"Today's exam revealed additional damage in Oscar's hip," Mom explains to Father Pete.

"But the car didn't hit me that hard," I say.

"This isn't from the car accident," says Dad. "It's from football, and it started months ago."

"You can't play football without getting hit," I tell my father.

"We understand that, Oscar."

Mom looks down and reads from the doctor's paperwork that's spread across our table. "Oscar has something called avascular necrosis. It can happen when an injury prevents blood from flowing to the bone that makes the ball part of the ball-and-socket hip joint. Bones need a steady supply of blood to stay healthy, so now—"

"The bone is dead," I say. "Part of my hip joint is dead, and it's not going to heal."

"Ever?" Father Pete asks.

"Never."

"There are surgical treatments that make it very likely that Oscar will be able to walk and even run without any problem in the future." Mom looks up from the medical report. "But no more football."

"I still might be able to play," I say.

"No," says Dad.

"But—"

"It is just a game, Oscar."

"It is not just a game," I say. "It's how I can go to college. It's how I can make a living. I can help you and Mom—"

Dad shakes his head. "We do not need that kind of help."

"You work in a pretzel factory!"

"What's wrong with the pretzel factory?" Dad says sternly. "I like my job. We make good pretzels."

"If I play football, you can have all the pretzels in the world," I insist. "We could buy our own pretzel factory if you want."

"This is not about pretzels," Mom hollers at me.

"I know that," I say. "It's about whether or not I can play football."

Father Pete clears his throat. "Is that what you think it's about, Oscar?"

All of a sudden, our conversation or argument or whatever this is comes to a sudden halt.

"Thanksgiving is next week," Father Pete says after a long moment. "Can you remember how you celebrated the holiday last year?"

So much has happened in the last few months. A year ago might as well be prehistoric times. "Who cares about last year?" I say.

"I care," Dad says quietly.

"We watched the Thanksgiving Day parade on television," Mom recalls. "After that we went to the football game."

"West Beacon beat Frackville, and then we came home and ate a lot of turkey," I say hurriedly. "The end."

"Carmen was already sick," Mom continues.

Dad reaches over and places a hand on her arm. "We didn't know that yet."

Mom closes her eyes. "She said she wasn't hungry. I scolded her for picking at her food."

I shake my head. "She was mad because you wouldn't make turkey tamales."

Mom sighs. "Tamales are so much work."

Suddenly, I remember that there is a message from Carmen scribbled on the underside of the table where we are sitting right now. I can't help myself. I start to laugh and cry at the same time.

"Oscar?" says Father Pete.

I shake my head. "This is not the way things are supposed to be."

"No," says Dad. "But this is the way it is."

CHAPTER 25

OSCAR

Father Pete comes back the next day and the next. He says a lot of things. I am sure they are good things. Just the same, I get under my blankets, and I stay there. On Thursday morning, I am at the kitchen table when Father Pete starts banging on the front door. "Oscar," he hollers. "Get out here!"

Mom and Dad already left for work because I promised that I would finally go to school today. I lied.

Father Pete rings the doorbell over and over until I finally let him in. "Are you ready for school?" he asks.

I know Mom and Dad are scared and worried about me. Honestly, I am scared and worried about me too, but I didn't think my parents would turn our priest into an attendance monitor.

"I'm going tomorrow," I tell him.

"Okay," says Father Pete.

I did not expect him to agree. "What?"

"Tomorrow is fine. Just come with me for a second."

Without waiting, he turns and heads back to our front porch.

I hesitate, but then I follow. The moment I step outside, something hits me in the chest and bounces away. "What was that?"

"What do you think?" Father Pete, who is just a few feet away, reaches into a mesh bag at his feet. He takes a football from the bag and throws a perfect spiral straight into my stomach. It nearly knocks the wind out of me.

"That hurt!"

"Good." He pitches another ball at me. "You said you'd go to school today."

I dodge, and the ball sails past my head. "I said I'll go tomorrow."

"You lied to your parents." He reaches into his bag, takes out another football, and sends it my way.

I catch this one. "Could you please stop?"

"Why should I?"

"I don't play football anymore," I blurt out.

"Neither do I."

I know Father Pete played Mighty Mighty Mules football with Coach Moyer about a million years ago, but we've never really talked about it.

"Did you know that I was one of the best high school receivers in the country?" he asks now.

"You were?"

He nods. "I got scholarship offers from everywhere."

"But you became a priest instead."

"First I went to play football for the University of Notre Dame."

I dodge another throw. "The Fighting Irish? Seriously?"

Father Pete grabs another football but surprises me by tossing it underhand. "I was a good Catholic boy. It was a dream come true."

This time, the ball comes my way in a slow easy arc. I don't mean to catch it, but the throw lands in the crook of my arm like a puzzle piece snapping into place. "How come I don't know this?"

"When I was in high school, I never faced anybody as good as me. Does that sound familiar?"

I don't reply.

"In college, I learned very quickly that the fastest kid in West Beacon is not the fastest kid in the country. I wasn't even the fastest kid on the team. My first year at Notre Dame I went up for a catch in practice, and a future NFL superstar swatted me down like a bug. It was a clean hit, but I got hurt, and that was the end of that. My big-time college football career ended before it began."

I toss the ball back to Father Pete. "And now you're going to tell me that getting hurt was the best thing that ever happened to you?"

"No," he says. "It was the worst. I dropped out of school. I was pretty lost. I fell away from my family. It was a terrible time."

"If this is a pep talk, it's the worst pep talk ever."

"I'm not giving you a pep talk. I'm making a prediction."

"You survived, so I will too? Things will get better? We'll all live happily ever after? Should I consider becoming a priest?"

Father Pete chucks a football hard into my stomach. "You're being a jerk, Oscar."

I know he's right, and I don't care.

"My prediction is that there is nothing you can throw that I can't catch."

I spent most of my career on the defensive side of the line, but I can still throw a football farther than most quarterbacks my age. "You wish."

"Try me." He points toward the cemetery at the end of the street. "I'll go long."

"You're wearing priest clothes," I point out.

"It's not the clothes that make the man."

"What makes a man?" I ask.

"Keeping your promises." He turns, heads off the porch, and jogs to the middle of the street. "You promised your parents you'd go to school today. I promise that there is nothing you can throw that I can't catch. If I can keep my promise, then you can keep yours."

I spin the football that's still in my hand. "This is ridiculous."

"I agree," he says. "You should be in school without me having to humiliate you."

"Fine." I follow Father Pete to the middle of the road. There is no traffic. In fact, the whole neighborhood is quiet and empty. "Let me know when you're ready."

The priest nods, then stretches both arms above his head. He jogs in place for a moment, then empties his pockets onto the hood of his station wagon, which is parked at the curb. Finally, he returns to the center of the street.

"Ready?" I say.

He nods. "You're going to throw that ball a mile, aren't you?"

"That's the plan."

He turns and looks toward the end of the block. "I'm going to have to sprint between two rows of parked cars, head through the cemetery gates, hop over a couple graves, and then make the catch without killing myself on a headstone."

"You're not going to make the catch."

"What if I do?" says Father Pete.

"It's not going to happen."

"Famous last words."

I take a closer look at the priest. Like I said, he's dressed in black pants, black shirt, black shoes, and a white collar. I guess that he's at least thirty-five, maybe even forty years old. But then, Tom Brady earned Super Bowl rings after he turned forty. Plus, Father Pete was good enough to play at Notre Dame and maybe even the pros. Still, I've never even seen the man go for a jog.

“If you make this catch,” I tell him, “I will go to school.”

“Promise?” he says.

“I promise.”

“You’re not lying to me?”

“I wouldn’t lie to a priest.”

“But you’d lie to your parents?”

“I’m sorry about that.”

“I forgive you.” He grins. “I can do that.”

“Are you ready?” I ask.

Father Pete crouches into a sprinter’s stance. “Ready.”

“Set?”

“Go!” Father Pete takes off. I drop back a little and watch him race down the street. He’s got an easy, loping gait, and it doesn’t look like he’s moving that fast. Still, he reaches the cemetery gate sooner than I expected. I bring the ball up, cock my arm, take two quick steps, and heave with all my might. I feel pain shoot through my leg and hip, but I ignore it. The pass sails over cars and porches and street signs. In the cemetery, Father Pete glances back over his shoulder. For a moment, it looks like he’s stumbled, but then I see that he’s hurdling over a gravestone. The ball is still high in the air, but it’s heading down now. Father Pete is at least fifty yards away. Even from this far, I can hear him laughing. A moment later, he raises both hands and makes the kind of over-the-shoulder grab that belongs on a highlight reel.

A half hour later, I slide into my clay class seat. Somehow, I feel like I have been cheated. Playing against a man with God on his side was never a good idea. Even winning couldn't end well. For better or worse, I don't need to worry about winning today.

CHAPTER 26

RILEY

Noah and I watch Mr. Martin reach into a large brown grocery bag that he's placed on a worktable at the front of the classroom. "Pay attention," he tells the class. "This is a quiz."

"There are quizzes in art class?" asks Aengus.

Mr. Martin nods. "They're called art quizzes."

Aengus points at the gray brick our teacher has removed from the paper bag. "That doesn't look like art."

"What about this?" Mr. Martin reaches back into the bag and takes out a pearl-colored vase shaped like a lopsided teardrop. A crack runs down the length of the piece like a lightning scar. Mostly porcelain white, it's got a burnt, brown tree bark pattern around its base.

"That one's better," says Aengus.

"Did you make the vase?" Noah asks our teacher.

Mr. Martin places the brick and the vase on his table. "I made them both."

Isabelia, who's sitting close to Mr. Martin, raises her hand. "I like the vase."

"It's got a crack in it," Aengus points out.

Isabelia shrugs. "I still like it."

"They are both made from the same stuff," Mr. Martin informs us.

"What stuff?" I ask.

"Riley," Noah says to me. "The class is called Introduction to Clay."

I give him an annoyed look. "But what exactly is clay?"

Mr. Martin raises an eyebrow. "That's a good question. Can anybody answer it?"

"You can," Aengus tells our teacher.

Mr. Martin takes a sip from a mug that resembles a circus clown with a handle stuck to its head. "Anybody else?"

Noah raises a hand. "It's mostly just dirt."

Mr. Martin lowers the mug. "Exactly."

"Was that the quiz?" I ask.

Just then, Oscar appears in the doorway. I exchange a quick glance with Noah. He and I ate with Mom and Uncle Pete at the West Beacon Diner last night. After dinner, Uncle Pete told us all about Oscar's injury. Uncle Pete also explained that Oscar's football career was probably over.

"Should you be telling us this?" Mom asked her brother.

"I'll go to confession later." Uncle Pete sipped from a cup of black coffee. "In the meantime, you need to promise that you'll keep it to yourselves. More importantly, you need to know that Oscar is going to need his friends."

"We're his friends," said Noah.

Uncle Pete stared at Noah and me over his coffee. "Sometimes," he said slowly, "it's hard to be friends with a person who feels like they've lost everything."

"There are quizzes in art class?" Oscar says now.

"They're called art quizzes," Aengus tells him.

Mr. Martin glances toward the door. "Nice of you to join us, Mr. Villanueva."

Oscar crosses the room and drops into the seat beside me.

"Are you okay?" I whisper.

He gives me an annoyed look. "Father Pete tricked me."

"He can be very tricky," I agree.

"He's supposed to be a priest," Oscar snaps at me.

I remember what Uncle Pete said. Still, I do not like Oscar's tone. Before I can say so, Mr. Martin lifts the brick and the vase above his head. "We've established that both pieces are made out of the same thing. And what is that thing?"

"Clay," says Isabelia.

"Which is?" Mr. Martin looks toward the back of the room.

"Dirt," says Aengus.

"Then which of these two pieces is better?"

"Is this the quiz?" asks Aengus.

"This is the quiz," says Mr. Martin.

"The vase is better," Isabelia says confidently.

"What if you want to build a chimney?" somebody calls out.

"Or what if you're one of those three little pigs trying to build a house that a wolf can't blow down?" asks Aengus.

"What if you don't like things that are cracked?" says Oscar.

Mr. Martin leans against his desk. "You're not pigs, and we're not building a chimney."

"The vase is pretty," I say.

Oscar shoots me a look. "The brick is useful."

I'm not sure, but I think we're having an argument.

Noah raises his hand again. "Is the vase raku?"

Mr. Martin nods. "It is."

"Ragu?" asks Isabelia.

"*Raku,*" says Mr. Martin. "It's a way of firing clay that includes several unpredictable elements in the process. You end up with a lot of mistakes, but the successes are often beautiful in unexpected ways."

He offers Isabelia the vase. She examines the piece for a moment, then passes it around. When it gets to me, I discover that the surface is cool and smooth, and the vase weighs almost nothing. I return it to Mr. Martin. "It really is beautiful."

"*Raku* is a Japanese term," Mr. Martin explains. "Roughly translated, it means 'happiness in the accident.' "

"I'm sick of accidents," Oscar says under his breath.

"Then you should look both ways before you cross the street," I tell him.

Noah kicks me under the table.

"What?" I say. "First he's mean to my uncle, and now he's going to say things about my mom."

"I was not—" Oscar stops, takes a deep breath, and then says, "I'm sorry."

"You should be," I tell him.

"Accidents happen," Mr. Martin continues. "Sometimes they are catastrophes. Sometimes they bring great gifts and beauty. Often, they are all of the above. In art and in life, accidents and surprises will shape us. For example—"

Mr. Martin takes his porcelain vase and stuffs it back into the paper sack. Next, he lifts the clay brick high over his head. Without warning, he brings the brick down on top of the bag with all his might. The art room is filled with the sudden, shocking sound of a ceramic vase exploding into a million tiny pieces. Mr. Martin, clearly proud of himself, hands the brick to Oscar while the rest of us stare at the man as if he's lost his mind.

"Did you really smash that vase?" I say.

"Didn't you see me smash the vase?"

"But it was really pretty. It was like real art. Why—"

"Accidents and surprises—"

Oscar cuts him off. "She's right. Why would you do that?"

"Why do you think?" Mr. Martin asks.

"You're trying to teach us something." Oscar sounds angry again.

Mr. Martin nods. "I am a teacher."

Oscar shakes his head. "Do you want us to think that broken things don't matter? If something gets ruined, we can just make it new?" His voice gets louder. "Like the world is just a big piece of clay we can mold into anything we want, so it's okay to waste things that are actually beautiful, and if bad things happen, we can just go back and fix them."

"That's not—"

"It doesn't work that way!"

The rest of the class, still a little stunned from the shattered vase, is silent. Mr. Martin, flustered and all alone at the front of the room, clearly doesn't know what to say or do next.

"Why doesn't it work that way?" Oscar asks now.

"I don't know," Mr. Martin admits.

"Then why do we listen to you?"

Our teacher does not reply.

"So which one is better?" Oscar asks after a long pause.

"Excuse me?" says Mr. Martin.

"The vase or the brick?"

"It's sort of a trick question," Aengus calls out from the back of the room.

Mr. Martin sighs. "It is sort of a trick question."

Oscar frowns. "I hate trick questions."

After that, everything happens very quickly. Oscar turns, lifts the brick that's still in his hand, and in one smooth motion he winds up like an All-Star pitcher. Without warning, he turns the clay block into a ninety-mile-per-hour fastball. The brick is still accelerating when it flies through the window at the back of the room. Oscar is gone before the last piece of broken glass hits the ground.

Somehow, the sound of glass bouncing off the floor, like Christmas chimes or jingle bells, brings me back to Philadelphia. I was holding two glasses filled with ice water when Mom handed money to the man with the gun. I remember condensation running down the glasses and dripping across the back of my hand. I couldn't move, and I started to shiver like I was freezing to death. Even after the robber left the restaurant, I still held on to the ice water. It wasn't until Mom slammed the cash register shut that I relaxed my grip. The two glasses slipped through my fingers and shattered at my feet. The sound made Mom jump. She stopped crying, turned quickly, and stared straight into my face. That's when she announced, "It's time for a change."

Suddenly, I realize that it wasn't a man with a gun that inspired my mom to make a change. It was me.

I jump to my feet. "I'm going after Oscar."

Around the room, our classmates remain quiet and confused. Aengus is standing and staring at the broken hole above his head. Isabelia is sitting up straight with her mouth wide open. Nobody knows what to do. I get it. But that's not me anymore.

I grab Noah's arm. "Come on!"

"I—"

"Uncle Pete warned us."

"I know, but—"

I turn to Mr. Martin. "We're going after Oscar."

The teacher nods. "Go!"

I pull Noah after me. In the hallway, I point at the set of double doors that lead outside. "This way!"

A moment later, we're in a small parking lot at the back of the school building. Nobody's there, but I see the brick. It's just a few feet away from the old pickup that Mr. Martin drives to school every day. The truck is so beat-up that I can't tell whether the brick hit it or not.

"I don't think he came this way," says Noah.

We turn back to the school building and discover that the exit doors have closed and locked behind us. Now we're trapped out here beneath a sky that's threatening rain.

I grab the brick. "Follow me."

Noah and I start the long jog toward the school's main

entrance. Less than a minute later, the clouds open and drench us both in freezing rain. We're still a hundred yards away from the front of the building when the wind picks up, and the rain turns into icy pellets. We try to run faster, but it doesn't matter. Water runs down my neck and back, and my socks feel like fat sponges. We finally stop beneath the overhang covering the school's entryway. Just then, the front doors open. Oscar steps outside. He stops when he sees us.

"This is yours," I say. Without thinking, I toss him the brick.

Oscar doesn't even try to make the catch. Instead, he watches the brick sail in a long, slow arc, smack onto the sidewalk, and then break into pieces. "I guess it is the same as the vase," he tells me.

"No," I say. "It's really not."

"They're made out of the same stuff."

"You're thinking about it wrong."

Oscar adjusts the giant backpack he's got hanging over one shoulder. "How do you know what I'm thinking, Riley?"

"You just threw a brick through a window. It's not like you're being subtle."

"The vase was something special," Noah says now.

"Raku." Oscar says the word as if it comes with a bad smell. "Happiness by accident."

"We're friends by accident," I point out.

Oscar shakes his head. "We're friends because you wouldn't leave me alone."

"You're welcome," I tell him.

"Oscar," says Noah. "You and I walked into the school office at about the same time, and that's all we had in common. Lucky scheduling is the only reason we ended up sticking together. Riley landed in West Beacon like an alien from the moon, and now she's one of us too. It's just one accident after another that brought us together."

"And the three of us have turned those accidents into something really good," I add.

"Not all the accidents have been good," Oscar says in a tired voice.

"Okay," I admit. "Not all of it, but—"

Oscar cuts me off. "Friends come and go. Bad things happen. Sometimes people die." He takes a big breath and then adds one more thing. "I'm tired, and I hurt."

I have to raise my voice over a gust of wind that blasts us with a sheet of rain. "That doesn't mean you should smash good things to pieces."

"That's what Mr. Martin did."

"That was just a vase."

The wind blows even harder. I wrap my arms around my chest and shiver.

"You should go inside," Oscar tells me.

"What about you?" Noah asks him.

"My parents are coming. I think I'm getting kicked out of school."

The three of us stand together without speaking for a long time. Then, without thinking, I step forward and wrap Oscar in a hug. My arms reach barely halfway around him, so it's sort of like hugging a house. "I'm sorry," I whisper.

He nods. "Me too."

I don't think either one of us knows what we're apologizing for.

Everything, I guess.

CHAPTER 27

NOAH

Riley and I return to the art room at the end of the day. We find Mr. Martin pushing a broom beneath a window that's now covered with cardboard and duct tape. "Didn't the custodian sweep all that?" I ask.

"It is very hard to clean broken glass," Mr. Martin says without looking up.

I point at a nearly invisible shard near his shoe. To pick it up, Mr. Martin reaches into a wet bucket and pulls out a tangerine-sized glob of clay. He presses the clump against the floor. The broken splinter plus dozens of tiny glass specks stick to the wet ball.

"That's smart," says Riley, who's wearing a Mighty Mighty Mules sweat suit that Mrs. James let her take out of lost and found. I'm in a pair of corduroy pants and a ruffled tuxedo shirt from the theater department costume closet. At least we're dry.

Mr. Martin glances at the clay in his hand. Covered with broken glass, it looks like a small lumpy diamond. "I get some things right. Sadly, not everything."

"You shouldn't have smashed the vase," Noah tells him.

Our teacher sighs and then drops the glass-covered clay into a trash bin. "I won't be doing that again," he promises.

"What's going to happen to Oscar?"

"Oscar is suspended for three days."

"Hasn't he missed enough school?" says Riley.

Mr. Martin nods. "I made the same point, but it was brought to my attention that throwing a brick in the classroom could be grounds for expulsion. Three days is generous."

"Are you mad at him?" Riley asks.

"I'm mad at myself. A better teacher would have handled things—"

"Better?" Riley suggests.

"Much better."

I follow Riley to the other side of the room, where we check out her most recent clay football. The piece has already been fired once in the kiln, so it's not really clay anymore. Now it's ceramic, and it's ready for glazing. Not only that, the sculpture looks like an actual football.

Together, we move Riley's work off the shelf and onto a nearby table. In the process, we accidentally bump into a big, handled vase, which happens to be mine. "Be careful," I say.

Riley reaches out to steady the vase. Instead, she knocks it into a fat glazed stegosaur. The dinosaur remains uninjured, but his ceramic horn punctures my work. My vase now includes several long cracks and a couple big holes too.

"I'm sorry!" Riley cries.

I sigh. "That was going to be for the art show."

"Can you fix it?" Riley asks.

"It was bone dry," I say.

Bone-dry clay has lost all its moisture and is ready for the kiln. It's also brittle, easy to crack, and very difficult to repair. Mr. Martin comes over and places two fingers on the damaged piece as if he's looking for a pulse. "It might not be dead yet," he announces.

"I liked that vase," I admit.

"You can try to fix it at home," the teacher suggests.

Riley and Mr. Martin help me pack the broken vase and the bone-dry shards into a cardboard box. "It just doesn't make sense," I say once we're finished up.

"I'm really sorry," Riley says again.

"I'm not talking about the vase. I'm talking about Oscar. A three-day suspension means he'll be back in school on Wednesday. That's the day before Thanksgiving. Why have him come back the day before Thanksgiving?"

Mr. Martin, who's returned to sweeping, turns my way and raises an eyebrow. "That's a very interesting observation."

"If I was a member of the Mighty Mighty Mules football team," Riley says slowly, "could I be suspended on the day before a game and still play?"

"As a matter of fact," says Mr. Martin, "you could not. However, your principal made sure that Oscar will be at school on Wednesday. She let us all know in no uncertain terms that Oscar will play in the Anthracite Bowl on Thanksgiving Day."

"But he won't be able to play," I say without thinking.

"Noah," says Mr. Martin, "the Anthracite Bowl is a very big deal around here. Especially this year. If West Beacon wins, the Mules are league champs, we get into the playoffs, and Mrs. Ballard still has a shot at her state championship."

"Plus we'd get to keep the big piece of coal in the lobby. I get it." I glance at Riley, who gives me a quick nod. "But—"

"Oscar can't play," she says.

Mr. Martin looks confused. "I don't understand."

I know we promised to keep the secret, but it sounds as if Oscar might actually play football one more time. Based on what Father Pete told us, that's a really bad idea. "The doctors let Oscar know that it's not safe for him to get hit anymore," I explain. "He might never play football again."

"He definitely can't play on Thanksgiving Day," says Riley.

Mr. Martin leans his broom against the wall. "Are you sure?"

"Very sure."

Mr. Martin crosses the room, closes the classroom door, and then returns. "Does anybody else know about this?"

"Oscar's parents," says Riley.

"And Father Pete," I add.

"What about Coach Moyer?" Mr. Martin asks.

I shake my head. "We don't know about that."

Our teacher leans against his desk. "Oscar could have been kicked out of school today, but his parents hardly said a thing during the discipline meeting. Instead, they came with Father Pete, and that's who did most of the talking. Father Pete insisted that Oscar should be part of the Thanksgiving Day game because it wouldn't be fair to punish the whole team with the state championship on the line. Mrs. Ballard ate it up with a spoon. I bet she believes that God is on her side."

"They lied to her," says Riley.

"*Lie* is a very strong word," says Mr. Martin. "Perhaps it's more accurate to say that they let Mrs. Ballard drink her own potion."

"You realize that potions come from witches?" I ask.

"If the pointy hat fits . . ." Mr. Martin crosses the room and retrieves his broom. "You're certain that Oscar can't play?"

Riley shakes her head. "Uncle Pete says it would take a miracle."

"Your uncle would be the local miracle expert. It's a miracle they're letting Oscar come back at all. Of course, that's not the miracle Mrs. Ballard is praying for."

"I don't think God helps with state championships," says Riley.

Mr. Martin leans on his broom and laughs. "Apparently Oscar Villanueva isn't going to help either. But how about the two of you give me a hand?"

"With what?" I ask.

Mr. Martin leads us to a long set of storage racks on the other side of the room. Dusty mugs and strange sculptures fill the wooden shelves. "It's time to get rid of some old work." He hands me a dirt-colored plate. "Make yourself useful and throw this away."

I examine the piece in my hand. It's not the worst plate I've ever seen. "What's wrong with it?"

"It's supposed to be a bowl."

"It's not a bowl."

"Exactly." Mr. Martin points at a nearby barrel, so I toss it in.

Riley grabs something that looks like a wine bottle with a neck shaped like a bent elephant trunk. "What about this?"

"Also not a bowl."

The elephant bottle joins the plate in the trash. I confess that the sound of smashing and crashing is kind of satisfying. Mr. Martin uses a toe to nudge a set of lumpy sculptures on the bottom shelf. "All the garden gnomes can go too."

The so-called garden gnomes look more like bowls

than some of the bowls, but Riley and I smash them all while Mr. Martin plays some old rock and roll on the classroom stereo.

"Destruction is art when it's set to music," he shouts over the volume.

"I disagree," Riley hollers back.

"Take it up with Pete Townshend."

"Who?" says Riley.

"Exactly," says Mr. Martin.

I hold up a shiny blue piece that might be a plate, or a tray, or maybe a really heavy Frisbee. "What's this supposed to be?"

"More trash," our teacher tells me.

"It's kind of pretty."

"So is motor oil in a puddle."

We empty several more shelves. I toss collapsed vases, lopsided candleholders, ugly pots, and many, many, many gnomes. Most of the pieces obviously belong in the garbage, but some of the work is kind of nice. Hidden at the back of one shelf, I find a shiny black cup with four tiny legs, a dragon's head, and a twisted tail for the handle.

"Is that really trash?" Riley asks.

Mr. Martin turns down the music, then takes the cup. "The tail is too long. The head's too wide. The legs don't match, and the whole thing wobbles. This is one broke-down dragon."

"It looks like A-plus work to me," Riley says a little defensively.

"It *is* A-plus work."

"How can it be A-plus work if it's broken?"

Mr. Martin takes the cup. "I remember the student who made this. She was trying to figure out the right proportions for the head and the tail, but she wasn't getting it. I told her that you generally learn more from doing things wrong than doing them right. She decided that it didn't make sense to wait around for those lessons to come by accident, so she went ahead and made this one badly on purpose."

"She tried to fail?" Riley asks.

"And she succeeded." Mr. Martin stares into the face of the dragon cup. "Afterward, she threw a perfect little teapot plus a set of matching cups. After graduation, she went on to art school."

"Is she an artist now?" I ask.

"I hope so," says Mr. Martin. "I also hope she's a doctor or a store owner or maybe even a teacher."

"Like you," I say.

"Let's hope that she's better than me." He studies the little dragon for another moment. "I've changed my mind. I'm going to keep this one."

"What for?" I ask.

"In honor of broken things." He places the little dragon on his desk. "They remind us that getting it wrong today does not mean we won't get it right tomorrow."

CHAPTER 28

OSCAR

I wish I hadn't thrown the brick. I don't mean that I regret the three-day suspension. Staying home is what I wanted in the first place. I just wish I hadn't screwed up in front of Mr. Martin, because there's still a lot I want to learn about clay. That's probably not going to happen now. I wasn't even allowed to attend class when I went back to school. I had to spend the Wednesday before Thanksgiving inside the tiny meeting room near Mrs. James again.

"It's in-school suspension," Mrs. Ballard informed me. "But you don't have to worry, Oscar. Missing class does not disqualify you from playing football as long as the absences take place while you're inside the school building."

I just nodded and said nothing. I wanted to tell the truth, but I didn't want Coach Moyer to get in trouble for trying to take care of me. Apparently, Coach and Father Pete have the same opinion as my parents when it comes to Mrs. Ballard. "She thinks God made oysters so principals could wear pearl earrings," Coach Moyer said before the meeting to decide my future.

"Am I the oyster?" I asked.

Coach shot me a look. "It's a metaphor, Oscar."

"Listen," Father Pete said to me and my parents. "Our goal is to keep Oscar from getting kicked out of school. We can make that happen by just letting Mrs. Ballard believe what she wants to believe." He turned to me. "She wants to believe that you can play football."

"But I can't," I reminded him.

"We are not going to talk about that," Father Pete told me. "You will apologize, and you will say nothing else."

"You want me to lie."

"I want you to say nothing."

"Like an oyster," said Coach Moyer.

"That's a simile," I muttered.

Coach actually laughed, but Mom kicked me under the table.

Mrs. Ballard and Mr. Martin entered the room a moment later. Mr. Martin tried to say nice things about me, but the principal cut him off. She was too busy swallowing Father Pete's story hook, line and sinker.

Honestly, people should have figured out that I wouldn't be able to play anymore. Between all the absences and then the crutches and finally the flying brick and the suspension, who in their right mind would let me play? But people believe what they want to believe. Apparently, people wanted to believe in me. The joke's on them. In the meantime, Coach Moyer made me promise to keep my injury a secret until Thanksgiving Day. "This might be the last gift football can give you," he said. "I suggest you take it."

Now Thanksgiving Day is here.

At our house, Thanksgiving starts with Apie pie for breakfast. Not apple. Apie. Depending on who you ask, Apie pie is Pennsylvania Dutch or Amish or maybe it's just a weird old coal country thing. It's sort of like a heavy cinnamon muffin the size of a baking dish. Mom and Carmen always made it together, so I'm surprised to find Dad pulling an Apie pie out of the oven when I wake up.

"What are you doing?" I ask him.

Dad places the hot dish on a towel at the center of our kitchen table. "It's Thanksgiving Day," he says simply.

"I know what day it is. Where's Mom?"

Dad ignores the question. He pours himself a cup of coffee, takes a piece of pie, and heads for the living room. "I'm turning on the television to watch the parade now."

The Macy's Thanksgiving Day parade—broadcast live from New York City—is another tradition Carmen insisted on. After that, it was always time to pack up and head out for Mighty Mighty Mules Football.

"I can't watch the parade without Carmen," I inform my father.

"Yes," he says. "You can."

The sound of marching bands, cheering crowds, and happy announcer voices tells me that he's found the right channel. I take a deep breath, slice a piece of pie for myself, and then join my father on the couch. He points at a huge inflatable clown floating over the streets of New York City. "I've always wanted to be one of those guys holding on to the balloon ropes in the parade."

This is something he says every year. "I know."

"They're called balloon wranglers."

"I know," I say again. I take a bite of Apie pie. It feels like I've filled my mouth with cinnamon and sand. "What happened to the pie?"

Dad tries his own piece. He chews, then forces himself to swallow. "I must have left something out."

"Why didn't Mom make it?"

"Your mother went to early Mass. She's going to spend some extra time at church, and then she's going straight to the football game."

"You didn't go with her?"

Dad nods at the television. "I like the parade."

I carry my plate into the kitchen and dump the rest of the Apie pie into the trash.

"I don't know what I'm waiting for," Dad says when I return to the living room.

"I don't know what you're talking about," I tell him.

"Balloon wrangling," he reminds me.

I drop back onto the couch. "Do you want to jump in the car and drive to the parade right now?"

His eyes narrow as if he might be angry, but then I realize he's considering it. Finally, he shakes his head. "New York is three hours away. Plus, you can't just show up. Balloon volunteers have to sign up a year ahead of time and then go to trainings and rehearsals too."

This takes me by surprise. "You've looked into this?"

"Carmen and I were thinking about doing it next year."

"What about me?" I ask.

"You always had football."

"Not anymore."

"Do you want me to sign us up?"

I turn and face my father. "For balloon wrangling?"

"Isn't that what we're talking about?"

We watch a crew of volunteers drag a huge inflatable Wimpy Kid into view. I rub my leg and wonder if I'll be able to walk the entire length of the Macy's Thanksgiving Day parade while holding on to a giant balloon. I guess there's only one way to find out. "Balloon wrangling sounds good."

"Okay," says Dad. "Now let's talk about today."

"What about it?" I ask.

My father keeps his eyes on the television screen. "Your principal thinks you're going to play."

"I want to play," I remind him.

"You can go to the game and tell her that. I will tell her that we have received additional information from your doctors and have decided to put your best interests ahead of hers."

"She is not going to be happy."

"Your mother will count Mrs. Ballard's heartache as a silver lining."

I can't argue with him there.

"You should still be with your team today, Oscar."

"What if I'm not?" I ask.

"I expect you'll get kicked out of school. You'll also put Coach Moyer and Father Pete in an uncomfortable situation."

"I don't want to do that."

"Neither do I," says Dad.

"I'll go to the game."

"Thank you." Dad points at a giant sock monkey balloon on our TV screen. "I will sign us up for next year's parade."

"Can we wrangle the sock monkey?"

"I'll see what I can do," Dad promises.

Together, we watch balloons and parade floats and marching bands pass by. I can imagine my sister getting excited about every single one. "This is hard without Carmen."

"It is," Dad agrees.

"Will it get easier?"

"I don't know," he admits.

"Then why are we doing it?"

My father takes a deep breath, then offers each word as if it is made from a crystal glass eggshell that might disintegrate at the lightest touch. "Memories slip away if you let them, Oscar." He pauses and then adds, "I want to remember."

I let a long time pass before I answer. "Me too."

Dad nods. "I know."

CHAPTER 29

NOAH

The house seems quiet and empty when I wake up on Thanksgiving morning, but there's half a pot of fresh coffee in the kitchen plus one slice of burnt bread sticking out of the toaster. I'm sure my mother has not planned any kind of feast for today, but I expected a little more than this. "Mom?" I call.

"In here, Noah!"

I find my mother in our garage pottery studio. She's wearing a pair of clean blue pajamas covered with pictures of cartoon farm animals. Her hair, usually pulled into a ponytail, is loose and long down her back. She's got a pair of wire-frame glasses balanced at the end of her nose. She looks younger this morning than she has in a long time. Maybe it's the tiny cows and pigs and chickens on her pants. Mom points at a table that holds my broken vase from school. "What happened there?"

"It lost a fight with a stegosaur."

"Fine," she says. "Don't tell me." She nods at Riley's football, which I brought home too. "If you get the glaze right, that's going to look just like that rock at your school."

"That's the plan," I tell her.

Mom turns to one of the mugs that Oscar, Riley, and I made. "Did you do this?"

"My friends helped."

She studies the piece more closely. "It's not done."

"Not yet."

"It's good work."

I know the mugs are good, but the compliment still takes me by surprise. It's the first really nice thing I've heard Mom say to anybody in months. "Thanks."

"Happy Thanksgiving." She puts the mug back on the shelf. "I didn't buy a turkey."

This is not a surprise. In the past, my father took care of the Thanksgiving turkey. He cooked it inside a weird metal contraption that looked like a cross between a barbecue grill and a fat tin rocket ship.

"Maybe there's turkey at the Beacon Diner today," I suggest.

"Are they open on Thanksgiving?"

"Sure," I say, even though I have absolutely no idea. "We can eat at the diner, and then go to the football game."

Mom looks uncertain. "I don't know—"

"Would you rather stay here and eat toast?"

"The diner sounds better than toast," she admits.

As it works out, the diner is definitely open. In fact,

they're offering an all-you-can-eat Thanksgiving buffet with turkey, mashed potatoes, stuffing, cranberry sauce, and breads, as well as a bunch of local specialties like bleenies, halupkies, haluskhi, and scrapple. There's also pumpkin pie, apple pie, and funny cake, which is a pie-shaped Pennsylvania Dutch thing made out of cake batter and chocolate. Long story short, Mom and I eat a lot of everything.

"I didn't know I was that hungry," Mom says when it's clear that neither one of us can take another bite.

"I haven't seen you eat anything except for coffee and toast since . . ." I stop because I don't want to ruin this good day by mentioning my father.

"I know." She plays with a coffee spoon for a moment. "I'm sorry."

This morning she gave me a compliment, and now she's offering an apology. Who is this woman, and what has she done with my mother? "It sounds like you're feeling better," I say carefully.

She nods. "I heard you working in the studio last week. It made me want . . ." She closes her eyes, then opens them again. "I wanted to join you. I wanted to meet your friends."

"You could have—"

Mom holds up a hand. "I didn't want to embarrass you."

"Isn't that what mothers are for?"

She smiles. "Next time."

"You're going to like them," I promise.

Once Mom finishes her coffee, we make our way out of the diner and back to our old minivan. We use the car for everything, so the inside smells like clay and pizza boxes and garden soil. "When is the last time you went to a football game?" I ask.

"I have no idea," she says. "I don't really like football."

"Neither do I," I admit.

Mom gives me a weird look. "Then why are we going to a football game?"

"For my friends."

She nods. "That's a good reason."

At the stadium, we work our way through the crowds and head for the stands. Cheerleaders and marching bands from both schools are already shouting and playing as loudly as possible. Even though it's Thanksgiving, people are still buying hot dogs and cocoa and popcorn. Despite the cold, the place feels like a summer carnival.

"Noah!" A voice comes from somewhere up above. "We saved you a seat!"

I look up and see Riley waving from the bleachers. She's sitting on the bench in front of her mother and Father Pete. Oscar's parents are there too. Mom and I climb the stands to join them. "This is my mother," I say.

Riley jumps up and gives my mom a hug.

"Oh, honey," Mom says. "I am not a hugger."

"Sorry!" Riley steps back. "I'll ask next time."

Mom smiles and shakes Riley's hand. "Next time I might say yes."

I take the spot next to Riley while Mom joins the row of parents right behind us. On the field, the Mighty Mighty Mules stretch and jog while the Frackville Golden Bears do the same in the opposite end zone. "Where's Oscar?" I say.

"Bad news," says Father Pete. "The doctors did not clear Oscar to play today."

Riley brings both hands to her face and gasps. "Oh, no!"

Maybe she's just a little too dramatic, because Father Pete smacks her on the head with a rolled-up program.

"Will Oscar sit with us?" I ask.

"Oscar will be on the sidelines with his team," says Mr. Villanueva, who is sitting behind me. "He is still a Mighty Mighty Mule."

"Go Mules!" says Father Pete.

Riley picks up a game-day program. The cover shows a cartoon mule wearing a football jersey facing off against a Golden Bear in a coal mining helmet. "Is everything around here about coal mining?" she asks.

The adults look at her as if she just asked whether or not there are actually bears in the woods. "Yes," Father Pete tells her.

"Even football?"

"Riley," says Father Pete. "This is called the Anthracite Bowl, and our mascot is the animal that literally pulled coal cars out of the ground. So yes. Even football." Without warning, he jumps to his feet and does a little jig in the stands. "GO! GO! GO! MIGHTY MIGHTY MULES!!"

The impromptu dance makes my mother laugh so hard that tears run down her face. I have seen and heard her cry so many times in these last weeks and months. I did not expect that her tears could be a sign that things might be getting better.

Riley's mom drags Father Pete back onto the bench. "Does anybody ever think that football might be too big a deal around here?" she asks her brother.

Mrs. Villanueva, who is leaning against her husband, offers a small, sad smile. "Only every single day."

We fall into an awkward silence that seems to last a long, long time. Finally, I can't take it anymore. "Anybody want a snack?" I ask.

"You didn't eat enough at the diner?" says Mom.

I rub my stomach. "I always have room for a hot dog."

Mom shakes her head. "The thought of a hot dog makes me want to throw up."

Riley, who's seated in front of my mother, hops to her feet. "Then I am definitely going with Noah."

I was hoping she'd say that.

"I'm getting a pickle on a stick," Riley announces when we reach the bottom of the bleachers.

"I'm not really hungry," I confess. "I just wanted to go for a walk."

Riley leads us to the line at the snack stand. "You don't want a pickle on a stick?"

"I don't want a pickle on a stick."

"They're dipped in chocolate," she says, as if this will make them sound more delicious.

"You want me to put a chocolate-covered pickle on top of the halupkies, and the haluskhi, and the funny cake that's already in my stomach?"

Riley buys two chocolate-covered pickles and hands one to me. "Nobody can resist a pickle on a stick."

I have to admit that a chocolate-covered pickle on a stick is delicious. It really has been a year of new experiences.

Back in the stands, we sing the national anthem and then cheer for the Mighty Mighty Mules as they kick off to Frackville's Golden Bears. While the crowd watches the action on the field, Riley points toward the West Beacon sidelines. Oscar, wearing a game jersey over his everyday clothes, is standing next to Mrs. Ballard, who's got her arms folded across the front of her own Mighty Mules sweatshirt. Neither one of them looks particularly happy. Meanwhile, a Frackville running back crashes through the Mules defensive line and scores.

"The Golden Bears take the lead!" an announcer bellows over the loudspeaker.

Mrs. Ballard looks even less happy now.

"What is a group of bears called?" I wonder out loud.

"A sleuth," Riley tells me.

I turn to face her. "How did you know that?"

"You're not the only person who knows things, Noah."

Father Pete laughs. "I think my housekeeper inspired Riley to learn more about the local wildlife."

"Mrs. Czarnecki?" says Riley's mother.

"Does she still hunt with a bow?" my mom asks.

"As it works out," Riley says a little defensively, "bears are really interesting."

Mrs. Baptiste leans toward Mom. "Riley told me about your pottery business. How's it going?"

"Oscar has been talking about it too," says Mrs. Villanueva. "Please call if you ever need help."

"Anytime," adds Mrs. Baptiste.

"Thank you," Mom says. "But—"

I cut her off. "We will."

Down below, our defense jogs off the field. Oscar wades into the crowd of helmeted players, who are obviously frustrated and upset. He finds Aengus, who just got bulldozed by a sleuth of Golden Bears. Oscar puts a hand on Aengus's shoulder and says something into the boy's ear. Even from the stands, we can see Aengus nod and straighten up a little. Behind me, Father Pete leans toward Mrs. and Mrs. Villanueva. "Oscar could be a very good coach one day."

Out of the corner of my eye, I see Mr. Villanueva take his wife's hand. "Oscar is a good boy," he says.

Four quarters and several chocolate-covered pickles later, Frackville's kicker hits a fifty-one-yard field goal on the last play of the game. The Golden Bears defeat the Mighty Mighty Mules to claim a Thanksgiving Day victory and the Anthracite Bowl Trophy.

Around us, West Beacon students and fans are shocked and heartbroken. Some of them are even crying. I want to stand and shout, IT WAS JUST A STUPID GAME, PEOPLE!

Since I don't want to get beat up, I keep that thought to myself. But also, I'm kind of sad and disappointed too. I guess I really wanted our team to win. I recall the words on Mr. Martin's bulletin board. Art is supposed to make you feel something. The Anthracite Bowl made us all feel something. I'm not saying football is a work of art, but maybe it's not just a stupid game either.

CHAPTER 30

RILEY

I'm still in bed when my phone rings on the Saturday after Thanksgiving. I answer without pushing the blankets off my head. "What?"

"Riley," says Noah. "We're making mugs. Bring help."

Mom, Uncle Pete, and I get to Noah's house less than an hour later. Oscar's already there with his parents. Mrs. Villanueva is setting up a coffeepot at the back of the garage. "If we're going to make mugs, we're going to need coffee," she announces.

I suppose that makes sense. Personally, I'd rather have chocolate-covered pickles.

"Thank you for coming," Mrs. Wright tells all of us a little nervously. "I've fallen behind this year."

"Arise, and go down to the potter's house," says Uncle Pete. "There I will let you hear my words. Thus sayeth the Lord."

Mom turns to him. "What are you talking about?"

He shrugs. "Jeremiah 18:2. It seemed like the right thing to say."

Mom socks her brother in the shoulder.

Oscar raises his hand as if we are in school. "Where should we start?"

Pretty quickly, Mrs. Wright and Noah get us all organized at separate tables and stations so that we can work on different tasks at the same time. Oscar and Noah start turning out new mugs on pottery wheels. Uncle Pete carries their finished work to drying racks. Mrs. Wright glazes pieces that are ready and preps them for the kiln. Meanwhile, Oscar's parents cut out cookie cutter shapes, while Mom and I make long coils of clay with a machine called an extruder. We lay the coils on a worktable and cut them into six-inch pieces that Noah will shape into coffee cup handles. When possible, we all take turns working in a corner that Mrs. Wright calls the Shipping Department. Basically, it's where finished pieces get packed in Bubble Wrap, stuffed into cardboard boxes, and labeled for mailing.

I remember Noah's story about the Bubble Wrap, and I start to laugh. "Can I use extra Bubble Wrap?" I ask him.

Noah grins. "You *are* the Bubble Wrap, Riley."

At some point, Mr. Villanueva joins Mom and me at our handle-making table. "Watch this," he says.

Mr. Villanueva cuts a two-foot length of clay, takes an end in each hand, and then sort of lassos, twists, and tosses the cord in one fluid motion. It lands on the table in a perfect pretzel shape.

"Show-off," Mrs. Villanueva says to her husband.

"You try," he tells Mom and me.

I study Mr. Villanueva's pretzel for a moment, then cut my own clay rope. I do the lasso, twist, and toss thing. Somehow, a perfect clay pretzel lands with a plop on the table in front of me. "I did it!"

Mr. Villanueva starts to clap. "You are a natural!"

I give him a huge smile because I am ridiculously proud of myself for making a big fake pretzel. "I've never been a natural before."

"Let me," says Mom. She picks up a piece of clay, balances it in her hands for a moment, and then copies what I did. After a couple tries, her pretzels look almost as good as mine.

"Excellent!" says Mr. Villanueva. "If you're looking for a job, the Lemko Pretzel Bakery is hiring."

"I'm happy at the diner," Mom tells him. "But maybe you can put Riley to work in a few years."

"I will plan on it," says Mr. Villanueva, who returns to the cookie cutter table with his wife.

Mom turns to me. "Maybe you have a future in pretzels."

"Maybe I have a future in West Beacon."

"Is that okay?" Mom asks.

"Go Mules," I say.

By mid-afternoon, I've lost count of how many mugs we've all made and how many bowls, vases, pots, and pieces we've packed for shipping. I know it's a lot.

"We've done enough for today," Mrs. Wright finally announces. "This has been a big help. Thank you."

"I'm having fun." My mother wipes clay on the old apron she's wearing over her shirt and jeans. "And I don't even know what I'm doing."

"That doesn't slow Riley down either." Noah lifts a big box onto one of the worktables. "See for yourself." He opens the lid and pulls out a coal-black football.

Uncle Pete gasps. "You stole the Anthracite Bowl Trophy?"

My mouth drops open. "Is that mine?"

I have to ask because the football really does look exactly like the carved block of stone that's supposed to be with the Frackville Golden Bears now. Noah lifts the football trophy straight over his head. "It's yours."

Somehow, Uncle Pete looks even more stunned. "That thing weighs over two hundred pounds!"

Noah poses with the ball held high in just one hand. "I am small but mighty!"

"You are small but dead if you drop that thing," says Oscar, who is still seated at a pottery wheel.

"Get over here and help me," Noah tells him.

Oscar holds up his hands. They're both covered in wet clay. "I'm in the middle of making something."

"What are you making?" Noah asks.

Oscar looks embarrassed, but then he removes a perfect little chess piece from his pottery wheel. He lifts it up so all of us can see.

"Oh," says Mrs. Villanueva. She grips the side of a table for a moment, then crosses the room and puts a hand on Oscar's shoulder.

"No more missing pieces," Oscar tells his mother.

She kisses Oscar on the head. "I wish that were true."

A pained look crosses Oscar's face. "I mean—"

"I know what you mean," says Mrs. Villanueva. "And I love you for it."

In the meantime, Noah is struggling beneath my clay football. The sculpture weighs less than a block of coal but more than a large bowling ball. Slowly, he lowers the trophy back onto the table.

"What exactly is that?" Uncle Pete asks.

"Riley made art," Noah explains.

I join Noah to get a better look at the finished piece. "It's a miracle," I say.

"I hope you don't mind," he says. "I dipped it in a black glaze, then fired it in the kiln after Thursday's football game so you could have it today."

I put a hand on the football. It really looks great. "I don't mind."

"This is definitely going in the art show," he tells me.

"What about your vase?" I ask.

He shrugs. "We can try."

Carefully, Noah retrieves another box and places it on a table. From inside, he removes the broken vase, a few clay shards, plus several extra pieces and tools. He lays everything out like a doctor preparing for surgery. Mrs. Wright joins us to look over her son's shoulder. "Fixing bone-dry clay is very difficult."

Noah nods. "I'm going to score the cracked edges with a needle, and then use a vinegar slip to attach the broken pieces."

"And then pray," says Mrs. Wright.

"Isn't that my line?" asks Uncle Pete.

With help from Oscar and me, Noah slowly repairs the cracks and holes in his vase. There are a couple spots that can't be fixed, so we cover them with the flat stars and hearts and footballs I made the last time we were here. "If we're lucky," Noah says, "everything will hold together when it fires in the kiln."

"Luck?" says Uncle Pete. "What happened to prayer?"

Noah offers a little shrug. "We'll take everything we can get."

Oscar and I press one last little football onto the vase while Noah keeps the piece steady. "What if this doesn't work?" Oscar asks.

Noah dabs a little more vinegary-smelling mud into a crack. "No matter what we do, this vase will always be broken. Eventually, it's going to fall apart. But that doesn't mean we can't try to make it beautiful for a little while."

I brush a bit of hair away from my face. "I guess this is what happens when you try to make beautiful things out of dirt."

"Ashes to ashes, and dust to dust," offers Uncle Pete.

Mom pokes him in the ribs.

"At least that's what I've heard," he adds.

I look closely at the vase, which still needs to be glazed and fired before it's even close to beautiful. It will be a miracle if it survives. Of course, it's sort of a miracle that it's still here at all, but then, looking around the room it strikes that me this is true for every single one of us.

"It's going to be okay," I say.

"How do you know?" asks Oscar.

"It's like Noah said. There are always going to be broken parts, but maybe dealing with the broken parts is what matters most."

Noah brushes over one more crack. "That works for me."

"And me," I say.

Oscar sighs. "I'll try to keep up."

"We'll catch you if you fall," I promise.

"You've already done that more than once," he reminds me.

Oscar is right. Of course, he and Noah have done the same for me, and I am sure that the three of us are not done falling down yet. We will try to catch each other, but sometimes we will fail. Sometimes we'll get hurt. Sometimes we will break. That's when we'll pick up the pieces. That's when we'll need each other most. Together—broken or not—we will help each other to get back up, and we will do it again and again and again and again.

Acknowledgments

While this story takes place in a made-up town, the setting is inspired by the people, places, schools, churches, and history of Pennsylvania's coal region. My friends and colleagues in and around Schuylkill County were especially important in bringing West Beacon to life. Special thanks to Father Leo Maletz from St. Matthew the Evangelist Catholic Church in Minersville, PA; Monsignor William Glosser, Pastor for St. Clare of Assisi Parish in St. Clair, PA; and Monsignor Tom Orsulak, Pastor for St. Peter the Apostle Parish in Reading, PA. Thanks also to the great people who run the Number 9 Coal Mine and Museum in Lansford, PA, where Father Tom is an outstanding (and very enthusiastic!) tour guide.

A very special thanks to my great friend John McLaughlin, who is a remarkable teacher, artist, and storyteller. He and his high school students welcomed me into their studio and helped me to understand some of the challenges, joys, frustrations, and possibilities that can come from working with clay. John also served as a guide and advisor for almost every pottery scene in this book. That said, any parts I got wrong are my own fault. Of course, I might have been distracted because John is one of the funniest people I know. Thank you, Johnny Mac!

Thanks also to Lauri Hornik and the entire team at Dial Books for Young Readers. I owe a special debt to Assistant Editor Rosie Ahmed; Copy Chief Regina Castillo; Designers Maria Fazio and Jenny Kelly; and wonderful artist Mary Kate McDevitt, whose work makes this book shine.

I am deeply grateful for the opportunity to create stories with my extraordinary editor, Nancy Mercado, and my fantastic agent, Susan Hawk. Your guidance, good humor, patience, and direction make my work better. Your friendship makes my life better.

Finally, I owe more to my family—especially my wife and best friend, Debbie—than I can ever adequately express. I love you all very much.